Growing Up With Secrets

Daniel Cory &

Charleine Shepherd

Copyright © Daniel Cory & Charleine Shepherd 2025

All Rights Reserved

No part of this publication may be reproduced, distributed, or transmitted in any form or by any means, including photocopying, recording, or other electronic or mechanical methods, without the author's prior written permission, except in the case of brief quotations embodied in critical reviews and certain other non-commercial uses permitted by copyright law. For permission requests, please get in touch with the author.

Dedication

We leave a special honour to name a character in our book in memory of a wonderful mum and special friend who sadly passed away in 2020. Forever in our hearts but still getting up to mischief in spirit with her friend Mumma D.

(Book Character - Shaz Jones)

In loving memory of

Sharon Baker (Shaz) - February 1959 to July 2020

A special honour to name another character from our book given to our friend Crystal who lives in the amazing state of Colorado, USA.

(Book Character - Crystal Johnson)

About The Author

Daniel began his journey studying the paranormal at 16 years old where he began looking into various books and websites. Later performing his first investigation over the local cemetery with his dog Kira, understanding how to use his gift to cross spirits over. Helped with knowing why some spirits remain earthbound and in April 2008 became the founder of Mystic Shadows Paranormal Team.

Joined by Charleine his close friend together with bringing life situations from investigating the paranormal world and how dealing with gay life was challenging. They wanted to show people living life without fear and be who you are.

Daniel discovered his psychic medium gifts from age of 5 and later in years to come, realising he was gay at 10 years old with both things becoming a hard kept secret it was difficult to deal with both things. To this day has continued helping people and spirits.

Charleine grew up learning her sexuality as a lesbian finding it a struggle but had the support of her wonderful mum and later learning about her psychic gift of clairsentience in 2017. She has been helped by Daniel's guidance to understand how to channel spirits and energy.

Growing Up With Secrets

CHAPTER 1

It was the 18th of May, 1991, the evening that Laura gave birth to Damian at 7:30 pm at the National Casgwent Hospital in South Wales. I'm Julia, Damian's grandmother, and I was the first to hold him. I couldn't help but sense that there was something very special about him. I felt the presence of my mother, who was in spirit, standing beside me while popping in to visit Damian.

As I looked down at him, I noticed he was observing everything in the room and showing no signs of crying. I turned to Laura and said, "This young lad is going to grow up very different."

"In what way?" Laura asked.

"Let's just say he will be a very talented young man!"

I left Damian in his mother's arms to allow them some bonding time and let the doctor run checks to ensure both were healthy. I stepped out of the room to find a payphone and call Marcus to tell him about the birth of his son.

Once I arrived at the payphone, I brought my purse out to get some loose change. Picking up the receiver and slotting in the coins, I dialled the number and waited for the ringing tone.

On the fourth ring, Marcus answered.

Daniel Cory & Charleine Shepherd

"Hello?" Marcus said.

"Hi, Marcus, it's Mum. Laura has given birth to a healthy baby boy!" I announced excitedly.

"No way! That's so amazing!" Marcus exclaimed.

"He is so special," I said happily.

"Mum, I can't wait to see him," Marcus replied.

"They'll be back soon. See you when I get home," I assured him.

"OK, see you later," Marcus said before hanging up.

Placing the receiver back on the holder, I began walking through the old creaky corridor towards the main entrance. As I got closer to the doors, I felt a cold breeze against my face, and the doors opened automatically.

Once outside, I took a deep breath of fresh air on this cold, frosty night. Out of the corner of my eye, I noticed a shadow. Turning to face it, I watched as the shadow slowly transformed into the spirit of a young woman with a head wound.

"Hello?" I called out, but there was no response.

Deciding to approach the spirit cautiously, I spoke gently, "I'm not going to harm you, I just want to help you!"

As I got closer, I asked, "What is your name?"

The girl hesitated before replying, "I'm Crystal."

Growing Up With Secrets

Just as I began introducing myself, I noticed the reflection of blue flashing lights. Turning towards them, I realised it was an ambulance. I glanced back at Crystal, but the girl had vanished.

Hearing the commotion near the emergency doors, I saw Crystal again, this time standing at the rear of the ambulance, watching as the stretcher was being pulled out. The girl was pleading with the paramedics, but they couldn't hear or see her.

As I passed the scene, I took a quick glance, shocked to see Crystal lying on the stretcher. Noticing the gunshot wound to the front right lobe of her head, I tried to get Crystal's attention. She responded, "I'm not leaving!"

With a heavy heart, I entered through the emergency doors and stopped at the vending machine to get a coffee. Taking a seat on the nearby bench, I sipped my drink while deep in thought.

Suddenly, to my surprise, Crystal appeared before me once more. Her expression showed worry and distress.

"What's happening?" she pleaded.

"The only way I can help is if you calm down," I said gently.

Crystal took a deep breath and steadied herself. I then asked, "Do you know where they've taken your body?"

Crystal shook her head. "I don't know."

"Go and see if you can find out where they went," I suggested.

"OK then," Crystal nodded before disappearing.

Making my way back to the maternity ward, I walked through the door. Laura looked up.

"You've been gone for some time," she remarked.

"I went outside to get some fresh air, and I was helping the spirit of a young girl," I replied.

Before Laura could say anything, the doctor walked into the ward, holding a clipboard.

"I have great news for you. Your blood test results came back all clear," he said with a reassuring smile.

"Oh, brilliant! I'm so pleased," Laura replied.

As she glanced over at me, she noticed a strange expression on my face. Before she could ask what was wrong, I turned and hurried out of the ward. Laura watched me leave, growing more worried by my unusual behaviour.

Meanwhile, in the corridor, I waited for Crystal to return with what she had found out. Facing forward, deep in thought, I suddenly felt a presence behind me.

"Hello, Julia," Crystal said.

Growing Up With Secrets

I jumped, spinning around quickly. "You gave me a right scare!" I exclaimed.

Crystal just laughed.

She then explained what she had discovered. Upon arrival, the ambulance crew had rushed her straight into the resuscitation unit. The hospital team had quickly moved her onto the hospital bed. One nurse began performing CPR, while another doctor placed electrode patches on her body to connect to the heart monitor.

"I didn't understand what they were doing," Crystal admitted. "I just saw them rushing around me."

I listened carefully, realising that Crystal was only beginning to understand what had happened to her. One of the nurses had announced that there was no pulse or heartbeat. Quickly, they brought over the cardiopulmonary resuscitation machine (CRM).

The doctor took the paddles, preparing to deliver a shock.

"Clear!" (First shock).

"Clear!" (Second shock).

"Clear!" (Third shock).

After receiving no response, the doctor in charge made the decision. She had been unresponsive for 20 minutes. At 8:45 pm, the doctor declared the time of death. The hospital team then began clearing up around the body, removing the medical equipment.

I turned to Crystal and gently explained, "The hospital staff weren't able to resuscitate you due to the extent of your gunshot injury."

Crystal looked at me anxiously. "What happens now?"

"I can help you move into the light," I reassured her.

"What is the light?" Crystal asked, confused.

"The light is where spirits move on to find peace when they pass from the physical world," I replied.

"I don't see the light," Crystal said worriedly.

"It's nothing to worry about. It might be because you have unfinished business," I explained.

"What could be my unfinished business?" Crystal asked, frowning.

"I'm not sure. There's not much we can do right now as it's getting late," I admitted.

"Is there any way you can help me?" Crystal asked hopefully.

"I will help, but I'll require a few days to figure out what needs to be done with your guidance," I replied.

"OK, thank you," Crystal said before vanishing.

Growing Up With Secrets

I sighed, glancing over at the clock. Visiting hours were almost over, and I needed to get back to the ward before leaving for home.

When I returned to the ward, Laura was waiting, her expression expectant. Sitting down in the chair beside her, she asked, "Where have you been?"

"The time was running out on the parking ticket," I replied.

"Oh," Laura said, with a confused look on her face.

I took the camera out and snapped a picture of Damian to show Marcus when I got home.

A nurse approached, smiling politely.

"I'm sorry, but visiting hours are over now. Mum and baby need their rest," she said kindly.

I nodded, packed away my things, and bent down, gently giving Damian a kiss on the forehead. Then I gave Laura a kiss on the cheek.

"I'll be back tomorrow to see you both," I mentioned to Laura.

"See you tomorrow," Laura replied.

Leaving the ward, I thanked the nurse and doctor for their help before making my way down the creaky corridor towards the main entrance. As I approached the doors, they opened automatically, and a blast of cold air passed by my face. I shivered, quickening my pace back towards the car. Unlocking the door, I got inside, started the engine, and waited for the car to warm up. I sat there for about 15 minutes before finally heading home.

Leaving the hospital car park, I drove along the deserted high street. There wasn't a soul in sight. I turned on the car stereo, playing some music from *Cher's Greatest Hits: 1965-1992* softly in the background. My mind was elsewhere, still thinking about everything that had happened with Crystal at the hospital.

Pulling up outside the driveway, I noticed Marcus's car parked there. Reaching over, I grabbed my bag off the passenger seat before getting out and locking the car door behind me. I walked up the pathway towards the front door, keeping the house keys in hand, feeling for the right one. Sliding the key into the lock, I turned it and pushed the door open.

"I'm home!" I called out while walking through to the living room, placing my bag down on the armchair.

Heading into the kitchen, I switched on the kettle. "Fancy a cup of tea, love?" I shouted to Marcus.

"Yes, please, Mum," he called back.

A moment later, Marcus walked into the kitchen.

"Mum, let me make the tea," he insisted. "You take a seat. It's been a very long day for you at the hospital."

Growing Up With Secrets

I sighed, sitting down. "Son, you have no idea what kind of day I've had."

I suddenly remembered the picture. "I do have something to show you," I said to Marcus. Getting up, I went to the living room, opened my bag, and pulled out the camera. Turning it on, I waited for it to load before scrolling to the picture of Laura holding Damian at the hospital.

"Take a look," I said, passing the camera to Marcus.

"Oh wow, Mum! He's so adorable!" Marcus beamed.

"Meet your son, Damian," I said warmly.

"When will they be home?" Marcus asked eagerly.

"They'll be discharged in two days," I replied.

"That's amazing. I can't wait to see Laura and meet my son properly," Marcus said excitedly.

Marcus finished making us both a cup of tea, passing one to me before sitting down at the table. As we started taking sips, he began asking questions about what had happened at the hospital.

"Were there any complications? How long was the labour? Did everything go smoothly? What did Damian weigh?"

I smiled. "No complications at all. Laura was in labour for about seven or eight hours. Everything went very well, and Damian weighed 7lbs 6oz, born at exactly 7:30 pm."

Marcus grinned, clearly thrilled. "I'm so proud of Laura for coping with the long labour. And I'm really happy that he's a perfect weight and healthy."

Glancing at the kitchen clock, I saw it was now 10:45 pm. I finished my tea and stood up, placing the empty cup in the sink to soak.

"I'm heading up to bed now, son," I said to Marcus.

"OK, Mum," Marcus replied.

"I'll see you in the morning. Goodnight," I said.

"Goodnight, see you in the morning, Mum," Marcus said.

I picked up my bag and made my way upstairs. It had been such a long day, and I couldn't wait to sleep. Once in the bedroom, I got myself ready for bed, turned on the bedside lamp, and switched off the main light. Sliding under the covers, I snuggled in, reaching over to turn off the lamp.

Within moments, I started drifting into a deep sleep, straight into dreams.

Growing Up With Secrets

CHAPTER 2

Waking up early on Sunday morning, I glance at the clock—it's 8:00 am. The sun is already shining through the window on the left side of my room. Stretching my body, I slowly get out of bed and walk over to the wardrobe to get my dressing gown, putting it on before heading to the bathroom. After using the toilet, I make my way downstairs to the kitchen, ready for my morning coffee.

As I enter the kitchen, I notice a note stuck to the fridge from Marcus:

Morning Mum,

Just a quick note to let you know I've left for work early.

I got called in for an emergency at 6:15 am at the funeral home.

I should be back home around 16:00. I'll sort dinner for us tonight.

See you later.

Lots of love,

Marcus xx

I switch on the kettle to boil, get my cup, and place a teaspoon of coffee inside. Heading over to the fridge, I take out the milk and prepare my drink. Once my coffee is ready, I place it on the table and

Daniel Cory & Charleine Shepherd

step outside to collect the morning paper. Returning to the kitchen, I sit down, slowly sipping my coffee while reading the newspaper.

After finishing my coffee, I place the cup in the sink to soak before heading upstairs for a shower. Now dressed and ready for the day, I make my way back downstairs, grab my bag and keys, and head out to the town centre to run errands.

Once in town, I stop at the cash machine to withdraw some money before heading to my favourite shop, Primark, to pick out a selection of baby clothes. I take my basket to the checkout, where the cashier scans everything and places the items into a bag.

"That's a total of £35.00, please," the cashier says.

I hand over £40.00 and politely ask, "Could I have the £5.00 back in change, please?"

"Of course, that's fine," she replies, counting out a mix of £1, 50p, 20p, and 10p coins before handing them to me. She also places the receipt into the bag.

"Thank you, have a nice day," I say.

"You're very welcome. Have a wonderful day," she replies with a smile.

Taking hold of my bag, I leave the shop and head towards Sainsbury's to get the weekly food shop. Upon arrival, I reach for a

Growing Up With Secrets

pound coin from my purse and insert it into the trolley coin slot to release it. I place the Primark bag in the trolley and head into the supermarket with my shopping list in hand.

Shopping List

- Bananas, Granny Smith apples
- Mixed grapes, satsuma oranges
- Tomatoes, cucumber
- Iceberg lettuce, mushrooms
- Potatoes, carrots, onions
- Cauliflower, broccoli
- Butter, milk, cheese, yoghurts
- Brown bread loaf, free-range eggs
- Fresh whole chicken
- Sugar, tea, coffee
- Biscuits (variety pack), breakfast cereal
- Jacob's cream crackers
- Mixed frozen veg, chips, Yorkshire puddings, potatoes
- Frozen chicken pieces
- Canned peas, carrots, sweetcorn, peaches, soup
- Andrex toilet rolls, shampoo & conditioner

- Baby milk formula, wipes & nappies

After gathering everything on my list, I make my way to the checkout and start placing the items on the conveyor belt. The cashier begins scanning them through to the bagging area.

"Good morning," I say with a smile.

"Good morning! Do you need any help today?" the cashier asks.

"No, thank you, I'll be okay," I reply.

Once everything is packed, I place the shopping into the trolley.

"That will be £65.74, please," the cashier tells me.

I take my debit card out from my purse and insert it into the card reader. After the payment is successful, the cashier hands me the receipt. I return the card to my purse and put it back into my handbag before pushing the trolley away from the checkout.

Feeling a bit hungry, I decide to stop by the supermarket café for something to eat and drink. Browsing the menu, I make my choice as a waitress approaches.

"Hello, what can I get for you?" she asks.

"Hello, could I have a cheese and pickle sandwich with a coffee, please?" I reply.

"Of course," she says, heading off towards the kitchen with my order.

Growing Up With Secrets

Ten minutes later, the waitress returns, placing the coffee and sandwich on the table.

"Thank you," I say, smiling.

"You're very welcome," she replies before walking away.

I take my time enjoying the delicious sandwich and sipping my coffee, appreciating the brief moment of relaxation. Once finished, I head over to the café till to pay, handing over a £10 note to the cashier. I wait while she places it in the till and counts out £5.20 in change before handing it to me.

"Thank you for stopping by. Have a nice day," she says.

"You too," I reply as I leave the café.

Making my way towards the exit, I step outside and walk through the car park to my car. Opening the boot, I unload the shopping from the trolley before returning it to the trolley bay and collecting my pound coin.

Driving out of the Sainsbury's car park, I head home. Pulling into the driveway, I turn off the engine, get out of the car, and unlock the front door. Returning to the boot, I pick up the shopping bags and take them straight to the kitchen. I put everything away in the fridge and cupboards before heading into the living room.

Placing the Primark bag on my armchair, I take out one babygrow and put it in my bag to take to the hospital later. Back in the kitchen, I pick up the notepad and pen, writing a quick note for Marcus and leaving it on the fridge.

Hey Son,

Left this note for you as I've gone to the hospital to see Laura and Damian.

Please can you prepare a Sunday roast for dinner? I bought a fresh chicken and other fresh ingredients while out shopping today.

I won't be home too late tonight. I'll aim for around 19:00 pm at the latest.

See you later.

Love,

Mum xxx

I place the note on the fridge, securing it with a magnet, then get myself and my bag ready to leave for the hospital. Picking up my keys and bag, I walk towards the front door. I open it and step outside, locking the door behind me before heading to the car. Getting in, I start the engine, put the car into reverse, and carefully back out of the driveway onto the road. Shifting into drive, I set off towards the hospital for visiting hours.

Growing Up With Secrets

Upon arriving at the hospital car park, I pull into a parking bay and retrieve some change from my purse. Getting out of the car, I walk over to the pay-and-display machine, purchase a ticket, and return to the car to place it on the dashboard. Reaching over for my bag, I close the door and lock the car before heading towards the main entrance.

Walking through the revolving doors, I make my way to WHSmith to pick up a few things for myself and Laura. The items I choose include cold drinks, puzzle books, crisps, a sandwich, chocolate bars, and a magazine. At the checkout, the cashier begins scanning the items and placing them into a bag. While waiting, I take my purse out of my bag.

"That will be £8.58, please," the cashier says.

I hand over a £10 note. He taps the amount into the till and presses enter. Taking out £1.42 in change, he places it on the counter along with the receipt. I pick up the coins and put them into my purse.

"Thank you, have a nice day," I say politely.

"You're welcome. Have a nice day too," he replies.

Taking the bag, I leave the shop and head through the main hospital area, glancing up at the direction board to find my way to the maternity ward. After spotting the correct route, I walk towards the lifts and press the button to call for the lift. When the lift doors open,

Daniel Cory & Charleine Shepherd

I step inside and press the button for the second floor. The doors close, and within moments, I arrive.

Stepping out of the lift, I follow the corridor leading to the maternity ward. As I push open the door, I immediately recognise the creaky corridor from last night's visit. Suddenly, an overwhelming, eerie feeling washes over me, making me shudder. As I walk further down the corridor, I have the unsettling feeling that someone is watching me.

At the other end, I notice a male spirit standing there with a mischievous grin. An uneasy feeling creeps over me. Without warning, he turns and vanishes through the doors. I continue walking down the corridor, but halfway down, I instinctively stop in my tracks. Looking over my shoulder, I check if anyone else is behind me. Seeing no one, I turn back around and take a few steps forward when suddenly, I hear—

"HELLLP!!"

A bloodcurdling scream echoes behind me.

I spin around quickly, my heart pounding, only to see Crystal standing there with a massive grin on her face.

Letting out a screech of pure fear, I exclaim, "Why would you do that to me?!"

Crystal bursts into hysterical laughter, unable to respond. Shaking my head, I turn and continue walking towards the doors. Just as I do, the male spirit reappears, stepping back through the door with that same notorious smirk.

Growing Up With Secrets

I decide to interact with the male spirit. "Who are you? Do you want my help?"

But he just continues standing there, his creepy smile unchanging, making no attempt to respond.

Choosing to ignore him, I continue to walk past him down the corridor and push through the doors into the maternity ward.

I walk over to Laura, greeting her with a kiss on the cheek.

"Hello, love, how is everything today? And how is my wonderful grandson?" I ask.

"Hello, Julia. Everything has been good today," Laura replies with a warm smile. "The doctor came around this morning and said we're both doing well. We'll be able to leave the hospital tomorrow morning. Damian is doing wonderfully—he's eating well."

I reach into my rucksack, pull out a carrier bag, and hand it over to her. Laura takes out the items and gasps.

"Oh my gosh, these are adorable! Thank you! We could put one on him now."

She dresses Damian in his new babygrow, then passes him over to me. I cradle him in my arms, savouring the moment—our special nanny-and-grandson cuddles.

"Marcus has been asking loads of questions about how you and the baby are doing. He's really excited for when you both come home."

Laura nods. "I can't wait either—to finally be home and start being a family."

Daniel Cory & Charleine Shepherd

She looks at me thoughtfully and says, "Julia, I have a couple of questions for you."

"Of course, what's on your mind?" I reply.

"Where did you keep disappearing to yesterday? And why did you look so shocked when you were in here?" she asks.

I hesitate for a moment before replying. "Do you really want the honest truth?"

Laura nods.

Taking a deep breath, I sit down in the chair beside her and begin explaining.

"After I left to make a phone call to Marcus and update him, I went outside for some fresh air. That's when I saw the spirit of a young woman standing in front of me. She looked confused and lost. I asked if she needed help, but she seemed unsure about what was happening. I heard the ambulance approaching. The moment I turned back around, she vanished, appearing near the ambulance as it stopped outside the emergency area.

She later appeared again inside the ward not long after I'd returned. That's why I rushed out into the corridor."

Laura's eyes widen. "Ohhh, so that's what was going on! Why didn't you just say that earlier?"

"I didn't want to worry you," I admit.

"I wouldn't have been worried, just concerned about you disappearing all the time," Laura says.

Growing Up With Secrets

"That's understandable. Sorry for worrying you," I reply.

I glance at my watch, noticing time is getting on.

"I'll have to leave soon. Marcus will be getting dinner ready."

"That's okay, no problem," she replies.

"I'll see you first thing tomorrow."

Gently giving a kiss on Damian's forehead before handing him back to Laura, I reach down for my rucksack and get ready to leave.

"I'll see you both tomorrow," I say.

"See you later," Laura replies.

Leaving the maternity ward, I make my way back to the car park and drive home, looking forward to a delicious Sunday roast dinner.

On Monday morning, I head back to the hospital to pick up Laura and baby Damian, taking them home to see Marcus, who is waiting and extra excited to finally see them.

CHAPTER 3

We pull up outside the house, arriving back from the hospital. The front door swings open, and Marcus comes running out, bursting with excitement to see us home and finally meet his son.

As I bring the car to a stop, Marcus can't wait any longer. He eagerly opens the rear car door to see Damian. Unclipping the seatbelt from around the baby carrier, he gazes at his son while Laura and I get out of the car.

We head inside, placing the bags down in the hallway before making our way to the living room to sit down.

I turn to Laura and Marcus. "Would you like a cup of tea or coffee?"

"A cup of tea, please," they both reply.

Heading into the kitchen, I take three cups from the cupboard, placing them onto the counter. Filling the kettle with water, I wait for it to boil. Suddenly, I sense a presence. I turn to find Crystal standing behind me, giggling.

"Crystal, it's not the best time right now. I'll call for you in a little while. I've just brought my grandson back home from the hospital, but I promise I'll help you later."

Growing Up With Secrets

"No problem at all, Julia," Crystal replies cheerfully before vanishing.

As she disappears, I finish making the tea and carry Laura and Marcus's cups into the living room. Returning to the kitchen, I pick up my own cup and then settle into my armchair.

I reach for the Primark bag beside me and hand it to Marcus and Laura.

"There's some more stuff I bought for you," I tell them.

Excitedly, they go through the baby items, their faces lighting up with joy.

"Thank you so much!" they exclaim in unison.

"I'll take the bags upstairs," Marcus says.

"OK, son. I'm just popping out to run some errands," I reply, watching as Marcus follows Laura upstairs, carrying Damian with her.

Once they've disappeared, I head into the kitchen and call for Crystal to return. She reappears instantly with a sarky grin.

"Yes? You called?" she teases.

I smile. "Yes, I did. Are you ready to sort some stuff out?"

Crystal nods eagerly. "Yes, I am."

I get a pen and notepad from the counter. "I'm ready to take down key details from what you tell me."

Notes – Crystal's Kidnap Situation

- One short male and three tall males

- Foreign accents

- Taken from the high street by a white van

- Location: Industrial estate in Rhondda Cynon Taf

- Cold and damp environment

- Partial registration plate: R217 (can't recall the rest)

- Old sign spotted: The Pump House, Tonypandy

Crystal places her hand on my shoulder and suddenly triggers a psychic vision, showing a brief yet harrowing glimpse of what happened to her.

She was kidnapped and taken to an abandoned warehouse on an industrial estate. Though part of the vision was hazy, I saw the sign 'The Pump House, Tonypandy'.

One of the tall men is on the phone, furiously demanding ransom money from Crystal's father. The only thing Crystal can hear is the rage-filled screams of one of her captors. The short man looms over her and forces her to scream, ensuring her father hears her distress over the phone. Then, one of the taller men storms over and punches Crystal in the stomach.

Growing Up With Secrets

Furious, the man on the phone throws the mobile handset to the ground after being told there will be no ransom payment. In a fit of rage, he pulls out a gun, presses it against Crystal's forehead, and pulls the trigger once.

(The vision ends.)

I exhale sharply, shaken by what I've just witnessed.

"Thank you for sharing that with me. This will help in finding some answers for you."

Crystal gives me a grateful nod before disappearing once again.

I get myself ready to head into town. Making my way to the front door, I call out, "Marcus, Laura, I'm leaving now. See you later!"

"OK, see you later," they reply.

I step outside, closing the door behind me as I unlock the car. After getting in, I start the engine and drive towards the town centre, looking for the nearest car park.

Upon arriving, I pull into a parking bay, turn off the engine, and step out, locking the car behind me. I head towards the shopping centre, taking the stairs down before making my way through to the library.

As I approach the library entrance, Crystal suddenly appears again, causing me to jump.

Daniel Cory & Charleine Shepherd

"Heyyy, watcha doing?" she asks playfully.

Without replying, I just give her a sarcastic look before walking past her and into the library.

Approaching the front desk, I ask the librarian, "Where can I find the section for the newspapers?"

"They're located on the right-hand side, second aisle," he replies.

Thanking him, I walk over and browse the shelves that have various dates on the boxes containing newspapers. I locate the box dated 19th May 1991. Lifting it down off the shelf, I carry it over to a table, place it down, and open the lid.

I pull out several newspapers, looking through them in search of relevant articles about Crystal's situation. Finally, I come across a few articles in each of the newspapers containing useful information.

One article in particular shows very detailed information:

THE SUN NEWSPAPER   19TH MAY 1991

YOUNG GIRL FOUND WITH GUNSHOT WOUND

A friend of the deceased came forward to share details of what happened on 18th May 1991.

She explained that, while walking down the high street with Crystal at 10:00 am, a white van suddenly pulled over, and two tall men dragged Crystal forcibly into the van.

Growing Up With Secrets

"As the van sped away, I managed to catch part of the number plate 'DLB'. After it disappeared around the corner, I rushed to a payphone and dialled '999'."

If you have any information relating to this case, please contact Crimestoppers on 0800 666 212.

I stare at the newspaper article, my heart pounding. This is Crystal's story—a real case, a real tragedy. And now, I have the first piece of the puzzle. I take out my notepad and review the information I have noted from the vision. As I continue searching through articles, I uncover more details related to the situation. I now have the location where the kidnappers held Crystal hostage before ultimately shooting her.

I move over to a computer and start researching the number plate of the white van, but I find no relevant information. Shifting my focus to the abandoned industrial estate, I check its exact location using digital road maps of the area and discover that it's about a half-hour drive from where I am. Gathering my notes, I place everything into my rucksack, log off the computer, and make my way out of the library.

I walk to the local police station and approach the reception desk, enquiring about speaking to the officer in charge of the kidnap and shooting case involving the young girl from the newspaper. The male

Daniel Cory & Charleine Shepherd

officer at reception asks me to take a seat while he calls someone down to meet me. A few minutes later, two officers arrive from CID.

"Hello, I'm D.I. Maddie Lopez, and this is my colleague D.C. Joe Gray. How can we help you this afternoon?"

"I may have some information regarding the kidnap and shooting of the young girl from the newspaper article."

D.I. Lopez leans forward. "And what information is that?"

"I've got the full number plate of the white van involved."

Lopez's eyes narrow. "How did you obtain this information?"

Now comes the complicated part—trying to explain how I got the number plate.

"Well... first, can I ask if either of you believe in the supernatural?"

Lopez and Gray exchange a glance, then D.C. Gray laughs. "I don't believe in that nonsense."

D.I. Lopez folds her arms. "Actually, I do believe the supernatural exists."

I smile. "That's good then."

Out of nowhere, Crystal suddenly appears, standing behind D.C. Gray.

"Heyyy, Julia," she says casually.

Growing Up With Secrets

"Hello, Crystal. Why do you keep appearing like that?" I reply with a sigh.

D.C. Gray frowns. "Who are you talking to?"

He glances around the interview room and is unable to see anyone.

"I'm talking to Crystal, the young woman who was kidnapped and shot on 18th May."

Lopez and Gray stiffen, shocked at my words.

"How do you know this Crystal girl?" D.C. Gray asks, his voice sceptical.

I take a deep breath. "I was at the hospital with my daughter-in-law while she was giving birth to my first grandson. After he was born, I stepped outside for some fresh air. That's when I noticed a young woman just standing there. I went over to ask if she needed help, only to realise she was in spirit."

Both officers remain silent as I continue.

"When the ambulance arrived, Crystal started to panic, realising that no one could see or hear her. I walked over and explained that when she was ready for some help, she could come to me and I'd do my best to assist her."

I pause, then glance at D.C. Gray.

"Just so you're both aware, Crystal is in the room with us right now. Standing behind you, Gray!"

Gray's expression freezes. "Er... er..." He stammers, his face going pale. Lopez, meanwhile, shivers. "I can feel a presence... it's gone ice cold in here."

Crystal smirks. "I like this Lopez person," she says, nodding towards Lopez.

I can't help but laugh. Crystal is enjoying this way too much. A moment later, she grabs Gray's hair and tugs it. Lopez giggles, watching his hair move as if by invisible hands. Crystal then pulls funny faces at Gray before poking Lopez in the side, making her jump.

I raise an eyebrow. "Now do you believe in spirits, Gray?"

Still looking shaken, Gray just nods.

Reaching into my rucksack, I retrieve my notepad and turn to the page with the number plate details. Handing it to Lopez, I watch as she carefully writes it down.

Lopez then asks, "Is there anything else Crystal can provide to help with the investigation?"

I glance at Crystal, who nods.

"All she remembers is that there were three men, two tall and one short. They were loan sharks."

Growing Up With Secrets

Crystal then reveals something even more disturbing. "This all happened because of her father. He borrowed money from them to gamble, but when they demanded repayment, he refused. That's when the short, chubby man punched Crystal in the stomach. The tall man got angry, pulled out a gun, and then shot her."

I sigh. "Unfortunately, that's all she can recall."

Lopez nods. "This is great information we didn't have before. Please tell Crystal thank you for helping us."

Crystal giggles. "No problem, I'm glad to help!"

Lopez says, "Thank you, Julia, for coming in and providing us with the new lead."

Leaving the police station, I make my way back to the car park. Reaching into my rucksack, I take out my keys, unlock the car, and get in. Taking out a map book, I find directions to 'The Pump House - Tonypandy', the abandoned location where Crystal was held hostage. Starting the engine, I pull out of the car park and begin my journey.

After a half-hour drive, I arrive at the abandoned site. I park the car, step out, and thoroughly look around at my surroundings. I have that feeling Crystal will appear any second, and the next moment, she appears behind me, making me jump yet again.

She bursts out laughing. "Julia, you're so easy to scare!"

Daniel Cory & Charleine Shepherd

I just shake my head. "One day, I'll get used to it."

Still grinning, Crystal points to a specific part of the building.

"That's where they took me," she says.

Walking over, I place my hand on the door, and it immediately triggers another vision. I see the white van pulling up. The three men step out, and one of the tall men opens the rear doors and drags Crystal out. She struggles, but they force her inside the warehouse, and the door slams shut. The vision ends. I leave the warehouse, go back to the car, get in, start the engine, and drive off home.

Growing Up With Secrets

CHAPTER 4

A few weeks later, the police contacted me and explained they had found the three men and the white van based on the information I provided. Crystal's father had also been arrested for being involved.

Crystal appears out of nowhere again. "Heyyy."

"Hey Crystal, I have some good news for you. The police have provided a recent update on their investigation. All three men involved have been arrested in connection with your murder, and your dad has also been taken into custody. The white van has been seized and placed at the impound for the forensics team to conduct their investigation."

"I'm really pleased they have been arrested, along with my dad," Crystal replies.

"Are you happy to cross over to the light now Crystal?"

"No, not yet, Julia. I would like to speak to my mother first, if that's ok? I must make sure she is doing ok after everything that's happened."

Sitting at the kitchen table with my cup of coffee, I ask Crystal if she can provide details about her mum. I reach for my notepad and pen, ready to write them down.

Daniel Cory & Charleine Shepherd

"My mum's name is Margaret Johnson, but she is known as 'MJ' for short. The address is 52 Sunrose Court, Newport, South Wales, NP25 6NQ," Crystal replies.

"Thank you for providing this. Let me check the A-Z map book to see how long it will take to drive to your mum's house."

It's going to take about a 20 minute drive. After finishing my coffee, I place the cup in the kitchen sink before heading to the living room to get my bag. I make my way to the front door and step outside.

Getting into the car, I start it up and begin my drive to Crystal's mum's house. I pull away, heading down the road towards the junction, where I turn left onto the high street. After about 15 minutes, the turn for Sunrose Court is approximately three minutes away. As I pull into the road, I spot house number 52, which has a blue Ford Escort parked in the driveway. Someone must be home.

Once again, out of nowhere, Crystal appears, making me jump.

"Heyyy Julia! That's my mum's car!"

"How many times do I have to explain it? Don't do that to me!!!"

"Sorrrry! I'm just so excited that I get to speak with my mum," Crystal replies.

"Hold on, let's take this one step at a time. I have to explain why I'm here, and I'm really unsure how she'll react."

Growing Up With Secrets

Pulling up outside the house, I turn off the car and get out, closing the door behind me. I glance over at the driveway and see Crystal already standing next to the front porch, looking very excited.

I open the front gate, walk up the pathway, and ring the doorbell, waiting for someone to answer. A woman opens the door.

"Hello, may I help you?" she asks.

"Hi, I'm a friend of your daughter, Crystal. My name is Julia Jones," I reply.

"Please come in, Julia. It's a pleasure to meet you. Take a seat while I put the kettle on to make us a cup of tea."

Margaret returns from the kitchen carrying a small tray with two cups and a plate of biscuits.

"How did you and Crystal become friends?" she asks.

"I didn't know her for very long. We happened to meet by chance under unexpected circumstances. May I ask you a question?"

"Of course you can," Margaret replies.

"Do you believe in the supernatural?"

"Not really, but why do you ask?"

"This might sound very strange to you. I have this special gift where I can see and speak to earthbound spirits."

Daniel Cory & Charleine Shepherd

"Is this some sort of joke? I have just recently lost my beautiful daughter, and you're preying on vulnerable people with this nonsense!!"

"I'm not doing this as a joke. Crystal is sitting next to me right now. She asked me to remind you about that special day when you both went out for lunch."

Margaret doesn't respond immediately. Her face is frozen in shock, possibly wondering how I could know that.

"How do you know about that?" she finally asks.

"Crystal also mentioned the special memory necklace she bought you for your birthday—the one you keep in the jewellery box on your dressing table."

Margaret's expression softens. "Wow... she's really here. I'm so sorry Julia, for being rude to you. I just miss Crystal so much. Sweetie, what happened to you?"

"Crystal says it's best not to tell you right away because it's a lot to process right now. She does miss you very much too," I explain.

Silence settles over us for a moment as Margaret reaches for a box of tissues, clearly overwhelmed by the situation. I give her a couple more minutes before continuing.

"I'm so sorry this is so distressing for you," I say gently.

Growing Up With Secrets

Margaret wipes her tears. "Can you tell Crystal how much I love her? She was the best thing that ever graced my life and everyone in the family with her kindness and wonderful smile."

"She can hear you. Crystal sends so much love back and wants you to know what a wonderful mum you were to her."

Margaret's voice trembles. "I love you too, Crystal. It won't be the same here without you, but I'm so glad I got to speak with you through Julia."

Crystal suddenly looks towards the living room door. "What is that light? Is this for me? I can see my Grandad waiting for me."

"Yes, it is. You're ready now."

Looking over at Margaret, I say, "She sees the light and mentions her Grandad is waiting."

Crystal turns back to me. "Thank you for all your help, Julia. Please look after my mum when I go. Tell her I love her so very much!"

Margaret wipes another tear from her cheek. "I love you too, sweetheart."

With that, the light grows brighter, and Crystal takes a step forward, ready to cross over.

"You are very welcome, and I'll let your mum know."

Crystal kisses her mum on the cheek—Margaret feels this as she touches her cheek. Then, Crystal walks towards the living room door, vanishing as she crosses into the light. There is a slight change in the air, a peaceful feeling that both Margaret and I notice as Crystal crosses over.

"Crystal has safely gone to the light and found peace," I say, looking at Margaret with a gentle smile. She wipes the tears as they roll down her cheeks.

I quickly pull out a small piece of paper and a pen from my pocket, jotting down my house number: 01633 721 960.

"Thank you for coming today and helping my daughter find peace. It's not going to be the same without Crystal walking through the front door when she visits."

"It will be strange not seeing her pop up out of nowhere and give me a fright, that's for sure!" I reply.

Margaret giggles.

"If you need to chat, here is my home number. Please give me a call," I say, handing over the piece of paper.

Taking a quick look at my watch, I realise it's time to head home and see my grandson. We both walk towards the front door. I give Margaret a quick hug goodbye before stepping outside.

Growing Up With Secrets

"Take care, Julia. Thank you again."

"You are very welcome. Call anytime if you need anything," I reply.

Walking over to my car, I take the keys out of my bag, unlock the door, and get in. Starting up the engine, I begin my drive home to see my family.

Arriving home, I walk through the front door, eager to spend time with Laura, Marcus, and Damian after a long day of running around to help Crystal find peace. It feels like I haven't even stopped to give my special grandson any attention over the last few days.

"I'm home, and I've brought us dinner!" I call out.

Laura and Marcus are in the living room watching TV while Damian plays with his baby toys, his little giggles filling the room.

Heading straight into the kitchen, I place the bag of food on the counter and open the cupboard to get three plates. Laura walks in to prepare a bottle of milk for Damian.

"Marcus, can you come give me a hand sorting out dinner, please?"

"Coming Mum," Marcus replies.

"I got us all fish and chips to make it an easy night, saves us from cooking! Marcus, can you dish out the chips while I do the fish?"

Marcus shouts, "Laura, would you like salt and vinegar on your chips?"

"Yes, please!" she replies.

We finish plating up the food, and I get three dinner trays from the cupboard, setting them on the counter. Marcus gets the cutlery and places everything neatly on the trays. He takes his tray into the living room while I bring Laura's.

When I walk in, Laura has just placed Damian in his baby seat after feeding and burping him. He looks up at me with a cheeky smile.

"What are you grinning at, my cheeky little devil?" I tease, leaning in to give him some attention.

Just then, I notice Damian's eyes aren't focused on me. He's looking past me towards the doorway, giggling loudly.

Marcus and Laura glance at me, wondering who he's giggling at. I turn around to see my mum standing there, making funny faces at Damian.

"Hello Julia. How are you, my love?"

I chuckle. "It's only Nanny Shaz making funny faces at Damian," I tell Marcus and Laura.

"Hi Mum, I'm ok. I was wondering why the little one was giggling. I didn't hear you pop in!"

Growing Up With Secrets

"How have things been with you, Mum? Haven't heard from you in a while. Who have you been haunting lately?" I joke.

"Well, no one of interest, to be honest. Just the usual," she replies with a smirk. "I'm doing alright. Thanks for asking, sweetie."

"That's good. We were just about to sit down for dinner when you suddenly made an appearance! Feels like a ghost magician show at the moment," I laugh.

Laura and Marcus remain silent, focused on their food, while Damian continues giggling as his Great Nanny Shaz fusses over him.

I quickly head back into the kitchen to fetch my dinner before it gets cold. Just as I approach the counter, I'm suddenly struck by a premonition.

I see the hospital—watching the two of us and Damian in his buggy, walking down the corridor. Then, the spirit of a man appears in front of me while Laura speaks to the receptionist.

Damian notices the spirit too and starts crying. I ask the male spirit, "You're the one I saw last time. What do you want? Do you require my help?"

The spirit just stands there grinning, making me feel uneasy. Then, he turns and walks towards the corridor. I whisper in Laura's ear, "I'm just going to follow this male spirit. I'll be right back."

Quickly, I follow the spirit as he stops near a signboard that reads:

Mortuary | Chapel of Rest | Doctors' Rooms 1-3

He pauses near Room 2. I ask again, "What do you want? Do you require my help?"

He finally replies, "I'm stuck here," then vanishes.

I turn back towards reception, where I see Laura sitting in the waiting area with Damian.

I walk over and take a seat next to her.

She asks, "What did that spirit want?"

"He's earthbound. He just mentioned that he's stuck and then vanished. Not very helpful—he kept looking at me with a creepy grin, just like the last time I was here."

The vision ended, leaving me with an uneasy feeling. I know it won't be long before we have to return to the hospital next week on Thursday, 31st June, for Laura and Damian's check-up.

I pull out a chair and sit at the table to eat my fish and chips, still thinking about the vision and wondering what could have triggered it. Something about that uneasy feeling doesn't seem entirely linked to the male spirit—I can't shake the sense that there's more to it.

Growing Up With Secrets

Marcus walks into the kitchen, carrying two empty plates on a dinner tray. I'm slowly eating when he asks, "Is everything ok, Mum? You look really puzzled."

"I'm feeling a bit unsure about our visit to the hospital next week after having that vision. I encountered the male spirit there, and something about it just doesn't sit right with me."

"Try not to let it bother you too much. It's probably nothing to worry about."

"Maybe, but I'm not convinced," I reply.

After finishing dinner, I put my plate in the sink and head back to the living room to spend some time with Damian before his bedtime. I notice he's giggling as Laura entertains him with a lion puppet, making different sounds and funny faces.

When he looks up at me, his excitement grows.

Laura smiles. "Are you ok? He always seems to love it when you walk into the room."

"Yes, I'm ok, love. He's so adorable."

I pick Damian up and settle into the armchair for a quick cuddle and some fuss.

From the kitchen, Marcus calls out, "Mum, Laura, do you both want a cuppa?"

We both reply, "Yes, please."

Laura hands me one of the children's storybooks we have a day trip to the zoo. I give Damian his dummy and open the book to read—it always soothes him before bedtime.

Marcus walks in with three cups of tea just as I turn to page two of the book. Damian is already relaxing, rubbing his eyes sleepily. By the time I reach page five, he's fast asleep. Gently, I hand the book back to Laura.

Marcus offers to take Damian from me and carries him upstairs to put him to bed. In the meantime, my mind is still occupied with thoughts of that premonition.

I reach down into my rucksack for a notepad and pen, jotting down quick notes about what I saw. Tomorrow, I'll head to the library to do some research, and maybe I can find something about the history of the hospital or any records related to this earthbound spirit.

Marcus returns downstairs. "Damian is sound asleep," he says quietly.

I glance at the clock and it's already 20:30 pm.

"I'll be heading to the library first thing in the morning to do some research. Looking to see if anything in the hospital's history links up with my vision tonight."

Growing Up With Secrets

"Ok, Mum, no problem," Marcus says. "I start work at 7:30 am tomorrow."

"Time for all of us to head to bed," I reply.

I take the three cups into the kitchen and place them in the sink.

"Goodnight, you two," I say.

"Goodnight," Laura and Marcus both reply.

Making my way upstairs and into my room, I climb into bed and switch off the bedside lamp.

CHAPTER 5

It's the morning of Thursday, 31st June. I'm sitting in my armchair, having a cup of coffee while Laura gets Damian ready before we head to the hospital for their check-up at 10:30 am. My mind is still occupied with the vision I had last week after how intense it was. I keep trying to figure out whether this male spirit actually wants help or if he's just messing with me, as he was from the previous few times I've been at the hospital.

Laura comes downstairs with Damian, all ready to leave. I take Damian from her while getting his bag and the pushchair ready. She takes the pushchair out to the car and places it in the boot. I put Damian into his car seat and carry him out to the car. After opening the back door, I secure the car seat in place and fasten the seatbelt around it.

Laura and I get into the car. As we pull out of the driveway, I can't shake that strange sensation that my vision is about to take place. The thought lingers in my mind as we drive towards the hospital.

As we approach the hospital's car park, a nervous feeling comes over me again. Laura notices my expression and places a reassuring hand on my arm.

"Don't worry, it'll be ok, Julia," she says.

Growing Up With Secrets

"I hope so. It's just a nervous feeling but probably nothing to worry about."

We drive around, searching for a parking space near the main entrance. Finally, we find one, and I pull in before turning off the engine. We both step out of the car. Laura retrieves the pushchair from the boot while I unstrap Damian from his car seat, lift him out, and place him into the pushchair.

After locking the car, we walk towards the hospital's main entrance. As we approach the reception desk, waiting for the receptionist to finish on the phone, suddenly I start to get an eerie sensation of being watched. I quickly glance around, but there's no one there.

The receptionist hangs up the phone, looks up at us, and says, "Good morning. How can I help?"

"I have an appointment at 10:30 a.m. Our names are Laura and Damian Jones," Laura replies.

"One moment… Yes, here it is. Please take a seat in the waiting area," the receptionist says.

"Thank you," Laura responds.

We take a seat while waiting for the doctor to call Laura and Damian in for their check-up.

Daniel Cory & Charleine Shepherd

I glance around, still unsettled by the sudden feeling that came over me at the reception desk.

Laura notices and asks, "Are you feeling ok Julia?"

"Yes, I'm doing alright," I reply.

The next moment, I spot the male spirit standing near the reception desk, with his usual creepy grin plastered on his face. Just as I process what I'm seeing, the doctor's voice echoes through the waiting area.

"Laura and Damian Jones."

We stand up, and I quickly whisper to Laura, "There's something I need to check on. I'll be back before your appointment is over."

"Ok, I'll see you after we come out," Laura says before heading into the doctor's room and closing the door behind her.

I turn and walk towards the corridor beside the reception desk, following the spirit's path. As I approach, I look up at the signboard again that reads:

Mortuary, Chapel of Rest, and Doctors' Rooms 1–3.

The male spirit gives me one last look before vanishing. Something compels me to continue down the corridor and step inside the Chapel of Rest.

As I open the door and enter, I see the male spirit standing with his back to me, facing the memorial table.

Growing Up With Secrets

He hears me approach, then slowly turns around to look at me… no longer showing that eerie grin on his face but looking sad.

I take a step forward. "What's your name, and why are you still earthbound?" I ask gently.

The male spirit hesitates before replying, "My name is Eric. I'm not quite ready to speak at the moment."

"It's nice to meet you, Eric. I understand that you're not ready to talk yet. Please come find me when you feel ready, I'd really like to help you find peace."

A moment later, he vanishes, leaving me standing alone in the chapel.

Curiosity kicks in. What was he looking at on the memorial table?

I walk over and discover an old photograph lying there. It shows a group of people on what appears to be a group holiday. Taking a closer look, I notice Eric standing in the middle of the group.

Turning the photo over, I find a handwritten date on the back:

April 17, 1975 – Miami Beach, USA.

This might be a clue to something I can research at the library.

I reach into my bag for my camera, take two quick snapshots of the photograph, and then put the camera away.

Daniel Cory & Charleine Shepherd

Turning around, I head towards the chapel door, opening it, walking out, and closing it behind me. I make my way back down the corridor to the waiting area.

Laura and Damian are still in the doctor's room when I arrive back, so I take a seat and wait for them to finish.

I glance up at the clock it reads **11:15 am.** I realise that nearly an hour has passed since **10:30 am,** when the doctor called them both in.

The next moment, the door begins to open, and I hear Laura say, "Thank you doctor. See you again soon."

She makes her way over to me in the waiting area.

"How was everything?" I ask.

"It was ok. Everything looked good. Here are the results from mine and Damian's checks," Laura says, handing me the test results.

"That's good. I'm glad everything went well with no complications," I reply.

As we begin walking towards the corridor, something on the noticeboard catches my attention. I stop for a moment to take a closer look. It's a flyer about the hospital's **memorial service on Tuesday, 17th July, at 19:00 pm.** I pull out my notepad from my rucksack and quickly write down details of the upcoming event.

Growing Up With Secrets

This gives me an idea. Maybe I can use this service as another way to learn more about the male spirit named Eric. I need to find out why that photograph was sitting on the memorial table. Hopefully, someone at the event will recognise the people in the picture or know something about Eric.

We continue making our way down the corridor towards the main entrance. As we approach, the doors slide open, and we exit into the car park, heading back to the car.

After strapping Damian in his car seat and putting away the pushchair in the boot, we have a quick chat and decide to go shopping for a few essential items.

"Why don't we stop at the supermarket café after we finish shopping and get a coffee and a bite to eat?" I suggest.

"That sounds like a plan," Laura replies.

When we arrive at the supermarket, I pull into a parking bay.

"I'll go get a trolley. Can you get Damian into his pushchair, please?" Laura asks.

"Of course, not a problem!" I reply.

We make our way inside, and I start thinking about what to make for dinner. Shepherd's pie sounds good, we haven't had that in a while.

As we walk through the aisles, I pick up the necessary ingredients while Laura picks up a few household essentials.

"Is there anything else we need while we're here?" I ask.

"That's everything for now. I can't think of anything else," Laura replies.

We head to the checkout and place our items on the conveyor belt.

"Good afternoon," the cashier says as she begins scanning our items.

I stand at the end, ready to place everything into bags. Once she finishes, she says, "The total comes to **£16.45.**"

I reach into my purse, take out a **£20** note, and hand it to her.

"Thank you," she says, tapping on the till before handing me back the change and receipt.

Laura takes the trolley over to place it in the secure trolley holding cupboard while I take Damian into the café to find a table. While waiting for Laura, I glance at the menu, debating what to order. Suddenly, I get a craving for an egg mayonnaise sandwich with red onion.

Laura arrives and sits down across from me. I hand her a menu.

"Have you decided what you're having?" she asks.

Growing Up With Secrets

"Yes, I'll have an egg mayo sandwich with red onion and a glass of orange juice," I reply.

Laura gets up to place our order while I take out a jar of baby food for Damian.

I scoop up small spoonful's and bring them to Damian's mouth, but he decides to slap it out of my hand, giggling as the food splatters onto the table. I pause for a moment, watching him laugh, then shake my head with a small smile.

"What was that all about, you cheeky monster?" I say playfully.

I pick up the spoon, clean it off, and try again. This time, he eats it.

Laura returns and sits down. "What's he giggling at?" she asks.

"Oh, just being a little monster. He decided to whack the spoon out of my hand a moment ago. I just managed to feed him another spoonful," I reply.

Laura laughs. "Damian is just like his dad when he was a baby! He's always had a playful nature."

I glance at Damian, who gives me a cheeky grin as I feed him the last of his food.

Just then, the waitress approaches our table with our food and drinks.

Daniel Cory & Charleine Shepherd

"Hello, I have an order for table 11," she says.

"Yes, that's us. Thank you," Laura replies.

I place Damian in his pushchair and give him his bottle, hoping he'll fall off to sleep. As we begin eating, I turn to Laura.

"What do you think about us all going away for a week's holiday? Maybe a Saturday to Saturday trip to Haven Holiday Park in Great Yarmouth?"

"That sounds like a wonderful idea. Let's have a chat with Marcus about it later tonight over dinner," Laura replies.

"That sounds good to me," I agree.

We finish our lunch and drinks. I glance down at Damian and see that he has fallen asleep with his bottle still in his mouth. Gently, I pull the bottle out and tuck it away in the bag.

We get ourselves ready to leave the café. Laura retrieves the trolley from the cupboard while I walk out with Damian in the pushchair. Together, we make our way towards the car.

I'm in the kitchen prepping the minced beef, onions, carrots, peas, mixed herbs, and some garlic. Laura walks in to make a cup of tea and asks, "Julia, would you like a cuppa?"

"Ohhh, that sounds like a lovely idea, thank you!" I reply.

Growing Up With Secrets

I continue prepping the potatoes, getting them ready to boil for the mashed potato topping. Everything is now prepared and ready to go in the oven. Glancing at the clock, I see it's 17:45 pm. By the time this shepherd's pie is cooked, Marcus will be walking through the front door from work. I remind myself that ten minutes before it's ready, I need to take it out of the oven to sprinkle some cheese on top before putting it back in to finish cooking.

As I'm tending to the shepherd's pie, I hear the front door open, followed by Marcus calling out, "Evening both! I'm home."

"Hello son! I'm in the kitchen and about to dish up dinner," I reply.

Laura calls out from the living room, "Hey honey!"

Marcus walks into the living room, gives Laura a kiss on the cheek, then picks up Damian for a cuddle before heading into the kitchen, with Laura following behind. Damian giggles as Marcus walks in and notices the table is already set with plates laid out. I bring the shepherd's pie dish over, placing it in the middle of the table. Marcus settles Damian into his highchair before pulling out a chair to sit down.

Laura asks, "Would either of you like a cold drink?"

"Yes, please, love," Marcus replies.

"Not for me, thank you, sweetie," I say.

I take my seat and serve myself some shepherd's pie. "I have something I'd like to talk to you both about—an idea I had. I wanted to get both your thoughts on it."

They both look at me and say, "What's that mum?"

"I was thinking about us going away on a family holiday for a week at Haven Holiday Park, from this Saturday to the following Saturday. What do you both think?"

Laura is the first to respond. "What a splendid idea!"

Marcus asks, "Do you have any dates in mind, mum? I'll need to double-check with work in advance."

Smiling to myself, knowing Marcus is in for a surprise, I say, "You don't need to worry about getting time off Marcus, it's already been sorted. We're leaving on 2nd July and returning home on 9th July."

Marcus looks at me, surprised. "How did you manage to get it all sorted before even telling me mum?"

"I have the mum touch, that's how!" I say with a grin. "So, is that a plan then Marcus? You don't need to worry about any of the payments. You just need your spending money because the holiday is on me, and it's all been paid for."

We continue chatting about the holiday as we finish dinner. Afterward, once everything is washed up, I head into the living room

Growing Up With Secrets

to sit down while we keep talking about our holiday trip. A moment later, the house phone rings.

"I'll get it," Marcus says, quickly getting up and heading into the hallway.

Marcus: "Hello?"

Antonio: "Hi Marcus, it's Antonio from work. How are you? Just a quick call—I've got some good news!"

Marcus: "I'm good! What's the news?"

Antonio: "I just wanted to say thank you for being such a hardworking and valued member of the team. We've received some wonderful feedback from clients recently about the amazing service you provided during the funerals."

Marcus: "It's a pleasure to be part of a great company and to serve our community."

Antonio: "With that in mind, I just want to say congratulations— we're promoting you to Head of Funeral Operations! It's an honour to pass on this wonderful news."

Marcus: "This is amazing! I can't believe it! Thank you so much. I look forward to taking on my new role."

Antonio: "You deserve it for all your hard work, Marcus. I'll see you on 10th July. Take care, bye for now."

Marcus: "See you then. Bye."

Marcus returns to the living room with a beaming smile and bursts out in excitement, "I've been given a promotion at work! I'm the new Head of Funeral Operations! This is amazing!"

"Well done, son! This is great news—very well deserved after all your hard work," I say proudly.

Laura adds, "Well done honey! I'm so proud of you. We can celebrate while we're away on Saturday."

Marcus is so excited about his promotion that he can't sit still. He decides to go put the kettle on to make tea for all of us. Meanwhile, I turn to Laura and say, "I'm thinking of getting a bottle of champagne so we can celebrate Marcus's promotion while we're at the caravan."

"That's a great idea!" Laura agrees.

"I'll pick one up tomorrow while I'm out getting some food for the trip. That way, we don't have to rely on takeout every night," I add.

With excitement in the air, we all get started on packing our bags, getting everything ready for our departure on Saturday.

I wake up on Friday, get myself together, and make my way downstairs into the kitchen. I put the kettle on, getting my cup and everything ready to make a coffee. Once the kettle has boiled, I prepare my drink and sit down at the kitchen table to make a list of things I

Growing Up With Secrets

need to get. While waiting for Laura and Damian to wake up so I can ask if she wants to come shopping with me, I pass the time by reading this morning's newspaper and doing a crossword puzzle.

Hearing movement from upstairs, I soon see Laura coming down the stairs and walking into the kitchen.

"Morning, Mum."

"Morning, love. The kettle just boiled if you fancy a cuppa."

"Yes, that would be amazing! Could you help me get Damian's bottle ready?"

"Already done, love. Prepped it about five minutes ago, ready for him."

"Wow, you work fast! Thank you!"

I smile and take a sip of my coffee. "I was wondering if you wanted to come with me to pick up some bits and pieces for the car journey tomorrow when we leave for Great Yarmouth?"

Laura thinks about it for a moment while I head upstairs to get Damian from his cot. As I approach his room, I hear him giggling, but then I also hear a female voice talking to him. Stopping in my tracks, I stand by the door, listening closely, trying to remember who it sounds like. Then it hits me like a ton of bricks—IT'S CRYSTAL!

I place my hand on the door handle, about to open it when suddenly, the room goes silent. Then, out of nowhere, I hear from behind me,

"HEYYYY JULIA!!"

I jump out of my skin in a panic. "Don't do that to me! Jeewizz woman! Are you trying to give me a fright?"

Crystal looks at me with a mischievous grin. "I'm sorrrrry."

Meanwhile, Damian is giggling away, enjoying the moment of madness.

"How are you doing, Crystal?" I ask, still recovering from the shock.

"I'm doing alright. Just learning different things about being in the spirit world. It's still quite new to me."

"You'll get there, it just takes time," I reassure her.

From downstairs, Laura calls out, "Mum, who are you talking to?"

"Oh, it's only Crystal! Be down in a moment, love," I reply.

I walk into Damian's bedroom, pick him up, and head back downstairs, only to realise Crystal has pulled one of her famous vanishing acts like a spirit version of Houdini! I chuckle to myself at her antics.

Growing Up With Secrets

When I reach the bottom of the stairs, I walk into the kitchen and find Crystal standing by the window, staring outside.

"Is everything ok?" I ask her.

She turns around and replies, "Yes, of course. I was just admiring the blue sky and the birds flying by."

Out of the corner of my eye, I notice Laura sitting at the table with a puzzled look on her face, as if she's thinking, *Who are you talking to?*

"Are you ok love? You look a bit shocked sitting there."

"Who are you talking to?" Laura asks hesitantly.

"It's only Crystal—the young lady I helped cross over a while ago. She came to check in on us. She was upstairs with Damian about ten minutes ago."

"Ohh! That's the one you helped cross over? I remember now," Laura replies.

"That's right, but she does love to pop up out of nowhere and spook the life out of me!" I glance over at Crystal, who is standing there with a massive smirk on her face.

Laura turns to me and says, "I'll come shopping with you, Mum."

"Ok love. Get yourself ready, and I'll get Damian sorted too."

CHAPTER 6

Laura goes and gets herself ready while I take Damian into the living room to change his nappy and get him dressed for our shopping trip. Once we are all ready, I get Damian into his car seat and take him out to the car while Laura locks up the house. We are all in the car, ready to head off to town. I glance in the rear view mirror and spot Crystal and my mother sitting next to Damian, thinking to myself, *This is what it's like having a female day trip into town!*

As we approach the car park in the town centre, I indicate left to pull into the multistory car park entrance, then stop at the barrier while I reach out of the window to press the button for a ticket. The barrier lifts, and I drive in, noticing a child and parent bay to the left. I pull into the space and turn the car off.

I get out to retrieve the buggy from the boot, then place Damian in it. After locking the car, we walk towards the entrance leading into the shopping centre precinct. Behind us, I hear my mother and Crystal chatting while Laura and I walk over to Primark.

I can't help but overhear their remarks about other shoppers as we pass them. I try hard not to laugh too loudly at their comments. Glancing over my shoulder, I see them giggling to each other. When

Growing Up With Secrets

we reach Primark, I quietly tell them both to behave themselves in the store. They just look at me, then at each other, and giggle.

I turn back and walk into the shop, and suddenly, I don't hear anything from them. As we browse, I spot the pair up to no good. Crystal is peering up women's dresses as they stand looking at clothing. I hear her say, "My, my, my! What dirty coloured knickers. That colour does not suit you, dear."

I struggle to hold back laughing, trying not to be too loud while feeling embarrassed at the same time. My mother, meanwhile, is looking under a lady's skirt, saying, "My, she does need some help choosing! Let's fling some of the polka dot knickers into her basket from over there."

I watch as Crystal and my mum walk past the polka dot knickers. The next minute, I see them both pick up a pair each, chucking them into the lady's basket as she passes by. I walk over to tell them both to behave, but they reply, "What's the fun in that?"

"It's not a playground for ghosts! Now behave, please."

They both vanish, leaving me standing there, wondering what on earth they will get up to next. I carry on walking to catch up with Laura and Damian, where she is looking at baby clothes. As I glance over, I spot them both reappearing in front of the changing rooms. They both look at me, flash a cheesy grin, and then walk inside as Crystal walks into the gents and my mother goes into the women's.

A few moments later, I hear Crystal shout to my mother, "Well, I'll be damned! This one is packing something interesting, Shaz! You should come and see!"

The next thing I see is my mother running from one side to the other like an erratic nutcase, full of excitement. I can't help but laugh to myself and quickly walk away before anyone notices. Then it dawns on me, realising I'm the only one who can see them both! Shaking my head, I walk back to Laura and Damian.

I haven't even bought anything for myself after spending the whole time trying and failing to keep those two under control. As we head towards the checkouts, I notice a lovely hoodie and decide to treat myself to one. After finishing at Primark, we walk back through the precinct towards Tesco to pick up some shopping for our car trip in the morning.

As we enter, Laura reaches for a basket. We walk around, picking up snacks and drinks for everyone. I head into the alcohol section to grab a bottle of champagne that Marcus doesn't know about. It's for celebrating his promotion. Once I've picked it out, I place it in the basket, and we make our way to the checkout. Laura places everything

Growing Up With Secrets

on the conveyor belt while I go to the other side to pack the bags after the items are scanned.

After finishing at Tesco, we walk out into the precinct and head back to the car park to drop off the shopping. I turn to Laura and ask, "Would you like to go to a café for some lunch?"

"Yeah, that would be great. I'm getting a tad hungry now."

As we walk, I think to myself, *There's a really nice little café in the precinct next to WHSmith called the Jolly Old Café.*

Laura opens the door, and I walk through with the pushchair, noticing a nice table by the window to the right. As we sit down, a waiter comes over and asks, "Would you like a highchair for the little one?"

"Yes, please. That would be very helpful."

The waiter walks away for a brief moment and then returns with a highchair for Damian.

"There you go. I will come back over in a moment to take your order."

"Thank you so much."

I reach down, unstrap Damian from the pushchair, pick him up, and place him in the highchair, strapping him in. Reaching over for the

Daniel Cory & Charleine Shepherd

menus, I pass one to Laura. We both glance at the menus, thinking about what we're going to have.

"I fancy a burger and chips today," Laura says.

"Great idea! I haven't had one of those in a while."

We look up as the waiter returns to take our order.

"What can I get for you both?"

"Could we both have a burger and chips, please? Also, a small bowl of scrambled egg and two glasses of Coke with ice."

"I've got that all down. I'll bring it over shortly for you."

"Thank you so much."

The next moment, we hear a commotion coming from the kitchen. Something flies past the doorway. I hear giggling as my mother and Crystal appear behind the counter, laughing. Dread fills me as I realise, they're causing havoc in here now.

I get up and walk over to the counter, whispering to them both, "YOU BOTH NEED TO STOP THIS!"

They just look me straight in the face and say, "It wasn't us throwing anything! We just spooked one of the kitchen staff."

Hearing two people approaching the counter, I quickly walk back to the table and sit down just as the waiter arrives with our drinks. He places them on the table before walking away.

Growing Up With Secrets

Laura looks at me. "What was all that commotion about?"

I sigh. "I really thought it was my mother and Crystal throwing stuff in the kitchen. Turns out they spooked one of the staff members, who ended up throwing something across the room."

"Oh, that's not good."

"No, it really isn't."

The waiter soon returns with our food and places the plates in front of us. We both thank him. While we eat, I feed Damian some of his scrambled egg. He sits there happily eating, then suddenly starts giggling out of nowhere. That's when I hear my mother and Crystal talking to him from behind me.

After finishing our meal, we get ready to head back to the car. As we walk through the precinct, I tell Laura to go ahead while I pop into a shop real quick. I make my way to Primark to look at the jumpers and T-shirts. Finding a few I like, I take them to the till, pay, and then head back to the car park.

Once we arrive home, we settle in to relax for the evening while waiting for Marcus to get back from work. We decide to order Chinese from the local Golden Dragon Chinese Takeaway.

Marcus returns home from work just after I phone through the order, while I walk into the kitchen and turn the oven on low to warm up the plates. I also get out the knives and forks ready. Returning to the living room, I continue watching TV and chatting with Marcus and Laura about our holiday tomorrow.

The doorbell rings, and Marcus goes to answer it.

"The food's here mum!" he calls out.

I walk into the kitchen, turn off the oven, and take the plates out.

"Could you help me dish up, son?"

"Yeah, of course mum."

We plate up the food. Marcus takes his and Laura's into the living room.

"Do you both want a drink?" I call out.

"Yes, please!" they reply.

As I begin pouring three glasses of Coke, a sudden sensation comes over me, triggering another vision. This time, I see myself sitting in the living room with Damian as he opens his fifth birthday presents.

He turns and asks me, "Nanny, why can I see ghosts and other children can't?"

The vision ends quickly, leaving me very puzzled. Placing the tray on the counter, I set down the glasses of Coke and my plate, then make

Growing Up With Secrets

my way back into the living room to have dinner. After we eat, we relax for the rest of the evening, watching TV before heading to bed.

It's Saturday morning, and we are all up early, ready to start our holiday. Marcus packs all the bags and Damian's buggy into the car while I gather the snacks and Damian's bottles. Laura takes Damian outside and straps him into his car seat.

I double check that everything in the house is turned off, pick up the last few things I need, and head out the door. Locking it behind me, I get into the back seat with Damian.

"Marcus, do you need to get fuel before we go?" I ask.

"Yeah mum, I do."

"Ok, make sure you fill it up, and I'll pay half towards it."

Marcus pulls into the petrol station and stops next to a pump. As he fills the tank, I watch the meter, then take out my purse and hand him some money so he can pay. He returns to the car after paying at the kiosk, then drives out of the petrol station, heading down the high street towards the motorway junction.

As we drive along the motorway, we listen to radio station Magic 105.4 FM. Some great hits from the 70s come on, and I find myself grooving to the music in the back seat.

Daniel Cory & Charleine Shepherd

We drive halfway before stopping to stretch our legs and get a hot drink at the Coventry Welcome Break Corley Southbound Services on the M6 motorway.

Marcus follows the signs to the car park and finds an empty space. After we get out, I retrieve Damian's buggy from the boot, place him in it, and click the straps in place. We all walk to the service station's main entrance.

Laura and Marcus head to the toilets while Damian and I wait for them. Marcus returns first and stays with Damian while I go to the ladies' toilet. When I come out, they're all standing there waiting for me.

We make our way over to the Little Chef restaurant. After finding a table, we take our seats, and Laura fetches a highchair for Damian. In the meantime, I reach for the menu and browse through it before the waitress arrives to take our order. The waitress walks over with a friendly smile.

"Hello there! What can I get for you?"

"Can we order two Meal 3s, one additional meal, a small bowl of scrambled eggs, three cups of coffee, and a small carton of apple juice, please?"

"Sure, no problem. Thank you for your order."

Growing Up With Secrets

She heads to the main counter, places the order slip on the kitchen clip, and then prepares our drinks. A moment later, she returns with them.

"Here are your coffees and the carton of juice. Your meals will be out shortly."

"That's great, thank you."

As she walks away to clean another table, we continue chatting about how exciting it is to be going on a Haven holiday.

Out of the corner of my eye, I suddenly notice a figure standing there, waving at me. I do a double take and realise it's Crystal, smiling and waving. Then, out of nowhere, my mother appears beside her.

I think to myself, "Oh my goodness, they had to turn up now!"

I mention to Marcus and Laura, "I'm just popping off to the bathroom. I'll be right back."

They both reply, "Ok," giving me the chance to slip away quickly and talk to those two mysterious troublemakers about behaving themselves, especially after their last performance at the café in the town centre.

As expected, they both appear in the toilets. I make sure no one else is around before speaking, not wanting anyone to think I've gone crazy talking to myself. Once I confirm the coast is clear, I begin explaining, "You two can't do anything here. I'm begging you this time, please!"

Crystal replies, "Ok, we won't. We promise."

"Thank you."

Opening the bathroom door, I make my way back to the table and notice that the food has arrived, and it looks delicious. We sit and eat while chatting. I glance over at Damian, seeing a huge smile on his face as he enjoys his food.

After finishing our meals and drinks, I head to the till to pay while Marcus and Laura take Damian outside. Once we're all back at the car, we continue our journey to Haven Holiday Park.

We finally arrive at the holiday park. As Marcus parks outside the reception building, I get out of the car and walk towards the office.

As I walk in through the main door, the receptionist greets me. "Good morning! How can I help?"

"Hello, I have a booking under Julia Jones."

"Could I take your booking reference, please?"

"Yes, the booking reference is JH55478."

"Perfect! I've found your booking. Three adults and one child with a cot. Let me get your key and a map of where your caravan is located. Here's your paperwork along with your night passes. You will be in

Growing Up With Secrets

Caravan Silver G311. Enjoy your stay with us at Haven Holiday Park!"

"Thank you so much."

Walking out of reception, I head back towards the car. Laura rolls down the window so I can hand over the map.

"I'll be right back, just popping into the shop to get some bits."

I walk over to the shop. Walking in, I pick up a basket and make my way down the aisles. I pick up some milk, tea bags, sugar, and a pack of biscuits, then head to the till to pay. Once I've paid, I walk back outside and get into the car.

Marcus has figured out where we're staying, and he starts driving towards the caravan.

After about ten minutes, we reach the caravan and park outside. We get out while Laura takes the key to unlock the door. Marcus gets all the bags from the boot, and I unstrap Damian from his car seat.

Once inside, Marcus and Laura take their bags to the double room at the end, while I place mine in the twin room. Returning to the kitchen, I fill the kettle with water, switch it on to boil, and prepare a nice cup of tea for us all with biscuits so we can relax after the long drive.

Daniel Cory & Charleine Shepherd

I also prepare a bottle for Damian, ready to settle in and enjoy the start of our holiday.

As the evening draws in, we sit together, chatting about where to go for something to eat or whether we should just get a takeaway. Looking through the small onsite brochure, we notice that there's a really nice restaurant at the holiday park, along with great evening entertainment.

We exchange glances for a brief moment before agreeing that it sounds like a great idea to try out the restaurant and then stop by the clubhouse for the evening entertainment.

We all get ready to go out for our meal at 19:00 pm. I dress Damian in his new outfit while Marcus and Laura finish getting ready. A few minutes later, they come out of their room, both nicely dressed and ready to go. Marcus retrieves the pushchair from the car, and I put Damian in before we head to the restaurant.

After finishing our meals, we make our way to the clubhouse, hearing the music echoing down the corridor. Laura and I search for a table while Marcus goes to the bar to get drinks. Once we find a free table, Marcus arrives with a tray of drinks. Damian, sitting in his buggy, claps and giggles with excitement.

I glance around as something catches my eye, and my next thought is:

Growing Up With Secrets

"OH MY GOD, HERE WE GO AGAIN!"

There they are, mother and Crystal dancing on stage like lunatics. No wonder Damian was so excited! A strange thought crosses my mind. I should call this "the chaos at its finest," with those two barmy mares pulling off their usual unexpected antics.

We stay for a few hours, enjoying the entertainment before finally heading back to the caravan.

After a fun night at the clubhouse, we return to the caravan to settle in. Before getting ready for bed, I make us all a cup of tea. We sip our drinks while watching some TV, then place our cups in the sink and head off to bed.

The next morning, I wake up and glance at the clock and it's 9:00 am. Thinking it's time to get up and get some things for breakfast, I quickly get myself ready and leave a written note before heading out:

Marcus, Laura,

Left this note to let you know I've driven into town for shopping, just in case you wonder where the car is.

That's if I'm not back by the time you wake up.

See you shortly.

Love Mum xxxx

I drive off in search of the local Sainsbury's supermarket. Pulling into the car park, I quickly find a space just a couple of minutes from the entrance. After locking the car, I get a trolley and head inside to pick up everything we'll need for the week.

After about an hour of shopping, I return to the car, load the bags into the boot, then return the trolley to the bay, and head back to Haven Holiday Park.

Upon arriving back at the caravan, I notice it's still very quiet. When I check in on everyone, they're all fast asleep—at 10:45 am.

Allowing them to sleep a little longer, I put the shopping away and begin preparing breakfast. Just as I start, I hear movement from the far bedroom, and the door opens.

Marcus steps out. "Morning Mum. You ok? Did you sleep all right?" he asks.

"Yes, love. I slept okay. I've been out shopping this morning while you all slept soundly. Help yourself to some breakfast."

A moment later, Laura walks out of the bedroom holding Damian.

"Morning, love. There's a cup of coffee ready for you and a bottle made for Damian," I say.

"Thanks mum. Could you sort Damian out for me while I have my coffee?" Laura asks.

Growing Up With Secrets

"Yes, of course I can," I reply, smiling as I take Damian into my arms.

While Laura and Marcus sit down to have their coffee and some breakfast, I take Damian down to the local beach for a bit. The air is warm this morning, with a blue sky, the sun shining, and a light breeze drifting through the air.

I place a towel down on the sand so we can sit while building sandcastles. As we sit there for about twenty minutes, I notice Damian suddenly drops his spade and bucket, staring intently at something. Curious, I turn to look in the same direction, wondering what has caught his attention.

All of a sudden, a woman appears, standing a short distance away, staring at us both with a distressed and confused expression.

I call out to her, "Are you ok? Do you need any help?"

She just stands there for a brief moment, staring at us with a lost look on her face. Then, in the blink of an eye, she vanishes, only to reappear right behind us.

"How are you able to see me?" she asks.

Turning around to face her, I reply, "My grandson and I have a special gift to see and speak with spirits. Can you tell me what happened to you?"

Daniel Cory & Charleine Shepherd

"I don't remember much. All I do remember is that I was beaten up by a group of men on a Friday night. I eventually got away and made my way towards the beach, hoping to find someone to help me. But I guess I was in such bad shape that I ended up in the sea. That's all I remember from that night… and now I'm here with you both."

Understanding what has happened to her, I quickly consider how to help her cross over into the light.

"Can you see the light?" I ask gently.

"Ohhh, is that what I'm seeing? Because I can see my great grandma and grandad waiting for me?" she says, her voice filled with surprise.

"Yes, they're waiting for you. It's ok. What you're seeing is a place of peace. Don't be afraid."

Without another word, she steps forward and crosses over into the light. I glance down at Damian, who looks puzzled by what just happened.

"You don't need to worry right now, little one," I say softly. "You'll understand it all as you get older."

For the rest of the week, we enjoy our time together as a family— spending days on the beach, exploring the town, playing in the arcades, and laughing together at the clubhouse in the evenings.

Growing Up With Secrets

On our last night before heading home, I take us all out for a meal at a nice restaurant. When we return to the caravan, we pack up our things, getting everything ready for our departure the following afternoon.

Daniel Cory & Charleine Shepherd

CHAPTER 7

We arrive back home on Sunday evening, just in time for dinner. We decide to order a takeaway, as it's easier than cooking a meal. I phone the local chippy to place an order for collection. Before heading out, I take my bags up to my room. I leave Marcus and Laura to warm the plates and set them out, ready for my return. It takes me all of five minutes to walk there and back.

When I return, I start dishing up the food and call them through to serve themselves. I finish plating mine and sprinkle salt and vinegar on my chips.

On Monday morning, I wake up and head downstairs to put the kettle on. I take a cup from the cupboard, add coffee, pour in the boiling water, and then add milk. With my coffee in hand I sit down at the table for ten minutes reading the morning newspaper, after finishing my coffee I make my way back upstairs to get ready for the day. Before I do anything else, I gather the laundry ready to take downstairs to put it in the washing machine.

While I'm upstairs in my room, thinking to myself before heading off to bed, I decide to look through my wardrobe. The next minute, out of nowhere, I hear two voices shout, **"WATCHA DOING?"** making

Growing Up With Secrets

me jump. I turn around to discover it's mother and Crystal appearing out of nowhere again.

I continue trying to decide what would be ideal to wear tomorrow for the hospital memorial service. After some searching, I come across a really nice peach coloured blouse that would go well with my black pinstriped suit. I pull both the suit and blouse out and hang them on the door, ready for the morning.

I get into bed and say goodnight to mother and Crystal as they both disappear, just like they always do. Lying down, I turn off my bedside lamp before resting my head on the pillow.

I wake up at 9 am, head downstairs to the kitchen, and put the kettle on. I take a cup from the cupboard, place a teaspoon of coffee inside, and get the milk ready. Once the kettle has boiled, I pour the water into my cup, adding the milk, and head to the living room. Taking a seat in my armchair, I switch on the TV to watch the morning breakfast show.

As I sip my coffee, I pick up the house phone and dial a number to book a taxi for 10:15 am. After hanging up, about ten minutes later, I hear light movement upstairs. The next moment, Marcus calls down to me.

"Mum can you make me a cup of coffee please?"

"Yes of course love. Shall I make a cuppa for Laura?"

"Yes please, and a bottle for Damian."

I get up from my chair and head back into the kitchen to reboil the kettle. While waiting, I prepare the cups for coffee and tea, then also get the bottle ready. Once the water has boiled, I pour it into the cups and add milk to both.

"Coffee and tea are on the kitchen table!" I call upstairs.

Finishing off my coffee, I realise it's time to head upstairs for a shower and get ready for the hospital memorial service, which starts at 10:45 am. As I reach the top of the stairs, I hear voices coming from in my room recognising them. A thought crosses my mind: *Oh no, they're back again!*

I walk into my room. "What are you two doing back here so soon?" Mother replies, "We've both come to support you at the hospital memorial service. We'll be good promise."

"You both better be! Will you help me with the gentleman who seems to be stuck here earthbound?"

"Yes, of course we'll help. That's why we came back this morning."

"Thank you both, it's much appreciated."

I head to the bathroom for a shower.

Growing Up With Secrets

After finishing my shower and drying off, I walk back into my bedroom, closing the door behind me. Before getting dressed, I plug in my hairdryer and start blow-drying my hair. Once finished, I put on my clothes ready for the day.

I glance at the clock and see that it's nearly time to leave. Taking one last look in the mirror, I step out of my room and head downstairs into the living room.

Marcus and Laura both comment on how lovely I look.

"Wow you look lovely mum," Marcus mentions.

"You certainly do look fabulous" Laura says.

"Thank you! I'm heading off to the hospital. I'll see you both later."

"See you later. Have a nice time," They respond back.

Opening the front door, I step outside and close it behind me. The taxi is already waiting at the front of the house.

I open the car door and get in. "Good morning."

The driver responds, "Good morning."

As the taxi pulls away from the house, we head towards the hospital.

Daniel Cory & Charleine Shepherd

Arriving at the hospital entrance, the taxi driver drops me off at the main entrance where the memorial service will take place. I pay the fare and say, "Thank you," before stepping out of the car.

Walking through the hospital doors and down the corridor, I suddenly notice the male spirit standing there with his back to me. He doesn't realise I'm approaching, and then, just as quickly as I see him, he vanishes.

Reaching the end of the corridor, I enter the main waiting area and walk up to the reception desk.

"Do I need to check in for the memorial service?" I ask.

The receptionist smiles. "Can I take your name, please?"

"It's Julia Jones."

"Thank you, you're signed in. Please head down the corridor to the memorial room where you'll find refreshments."

I make my way down the short corridor and step into the room where the memorial service is being held. I notice a few people already there, sitting and chatting since we've all arrived early.

Helping myself to a cup of ready-made coffee and a couple of biscuits, I take a seat next to a woman who turns to me with a warm smile.

"Hello, nice to meet you. My name is Lucy."

Growing Up With Secrets

"Hello Lucy, it's a pleasure to meet you too. I'm Julia."

We start chatting briefly about the service, remembering all the loved ones and friends who passed during World War II. As we talk, my thoughts drift to the male spirit. *Could he have been one of the soldiers killed in the war?* I wonder. *But why is he still earthbound? Why does he refuse to speak to me?*

Since I first started visiting this hospital, he has appeared to me frequently. I can't make sense of it yet, but something tells me there's more to uncover.

A voice interrupts my thoughts as we're all asked to take our seats, now the ceremony is about to begin. I glance toward the table and see the male spirit standing there, looking around the room. His gaze eventually lands on me. He gives me a half-smile.

I smile back.

Then turning his back to me, he focuses on the speaker at the front of the room.

The speaker continues to read the names in remembrance of those who gave their lives during World War II. As they move through the short list, I notice a sudden reaction from the male spirit when the next name is read out:

Daniel Cory & Charleine Shepherd

"Lieutenant Julian Hammonsworth – 2nd Regiment, squad flyer. Collided with a German aircraft during a night patrol."

Julian becomes visibly agitated by what is being said. He starts shouting at the speaker, but they cannot hear him. Then in a sudden burst of energy, he vanishes—just as two of the lights blow out.

For a brief moment, the entire room is in shock. People glance around, likely wondering what just happened. After a few murmurs, the speaker regains composure and continues reading the final name on the list before moving on to the closing speech. They express gratitude to everyone for attending, honouring all those who served in World War II, and officially bringing the memorial service to a close.

As people begin to gather their belongings, I notice a photograph still sitting on the table. I approach the memorial service organiser and ask if I may borrow it, explaining that one of the people in the photograph was known by someone in my family. She agrees, and just as I'm about to leave the room, Crystal suddenly appears out of nowhere, a look of worry on her face.

Luckily, the organiser has just walked out, so I take the opportunity to ask Crystal what's wrong.

"We've located Julian. He's in the old part of the hospital that's been closed off. Your mum is with him in the abandoned mortuary. Come quickly!"

Growing Up With Secrets

"Do you know how he's feeling now?" I ask.

"He's calmed down since earlier when you saw him. The mortuary is the only place he's been aware of since passing away in the war."

"Let's go Crystal. You'll have to show me the way to the old mortuary."

Leaving the memorial room, I follow Crystal down a corridor where an old signboard marks the entrance to the disused section of the hospital. We push through a set of swing doors, entering a dark corridor so I reach into my handbag to pull out a pocket torch and turn it on. . The air feels heavy, with the atmosphere unsettling. Passing through more corridors and seeing a lift, Crystal directs me towards the last corridor on the right.

We reach the long, dark, and eerie corridor, walking cautiously until we arrive at the doors of the abandoned mortuary. The cold stillness of the place sends a chill down my spine.

As I step inside, shining the torch as I glance around at the old fridges that once stored the deceased. My eyes catch sight of another door, slightly ajar. From within, I hear my mother's voice. I walk over and gently push it open.

Inside, Julian stands before my mum, listening intently as she speaks to him.

"Hi mum," I say.

She turns around and smiles. "Hello love. Let me introduce you both. Julia, this is Julian."

I step forward. "Hello Julian, it's nice to meet you."

"It's nice to meet you too Julia. I want to apologise for making things difficult earlier and not communicating with you before."

"It's ok. How can I help you cross over into the light and find peace?"

Julian hesitates for a moment before speaking. "I just want to know what happened to me."

Taking a deep breath, I explain, "From the research I've done, a German bomber plane collided with your Spitfire in October 1939. Sadly, you died instantly on impact, and you were brought to this hospital."

Julian listens intently, his expression shifting as the realisation sinks in. "I remember flying that day, but I don't remember anything after that. Now I understand what happened." His eyes widen slightly. "Is that light for me? I can see my wife and children waiting for me."

I smile softly. "Yes Julian. That is the light for you. Its place that will help you find peace."

Growing Up With Secrets

A look of relief washes over his face. "Thank you for helping me. And I'm truly sorry for any trouble I caused before."

"It's ok. Take care of yourself," I say gently.

I watch as Julian steps towards the doorway. The moment he crosses over, he vanishes, leaving behind a profound sense of calm. The air, once heavy with sorrow, now feels lighter and more peaceful.

I turn to my mother and Crystal with a smirk. "Right, you two troublemakers, help me out of here before I end up getting into trouble myself!"

CHAPTER 8

The last two years have passed by quickly, and now it's July 1993. Looking back, I remember the memorial service at the hospital and reflect on it being the last time I saw Julian Hammonsworth, the troubled earthbound spirit whom I helped cross over into the light from the old hospital morgue. It was a very strange year, filled with several unusual situations involving Crystal and Julian.

Crystal is still around, performing her usual tricks of making me jump when she suddenly appears from nowhere. She has become very close to Damian as he gets older. Over the last few months, she has been helping him learn how to speak to spirits, which is amazing because now he has the same ability as me.

It's hard to believe how much Damian has grown—he's now two years old. Things have been difficult recently, especially with Marcus and Laura going their separate ways and preparing for their divorce. The house feels quiet on certain days, especially now that Damian is living with Laura and her new partner full-time. I'm not entirely sure about this new man she's seeing; there's something strange about his energy. Over time, I suppose more will be revealed.

We get to see Damian twice a week and every other weekend.

Growing Up With Secrets

Marcus has continued his work at the funeral care centre and was promoted to Funeral Operations Director six months ago for his hard work and determination. He and his team have even been featured in the local community newsletter, with the company being recognised as the top funeral service provider in South Wales.

Right now, I'm sitting in my armchair, sipping a cup of tea and thinking about everything that's happened over the past few weeks. Suddenly, something catches my eye, seeing something pass by the living room door. Placing my cup on the table, I get up and head towards the kitchen, hoping that no one is going to give me a fright by appearing behind me.

When I enter the kitchen, I find mother and Crystal standing there. In my head I think, *Here we go again. What are they up to now?*

"Hello Julia. How are you doing sweetie? Is everything ok?" my mum asks.

I glance at her and reply, "It's not the same. Things have changed since Laura and Damian moved out. Marcus and I are just taking it day by day for now. What brings you both here?"

"We were just popping in to see how you were."

"Thank you for not making me jump this time, Crystal!"

"That's alright Julia. I know things have been tough recently. I didn't want to upset you," Crystal says.

"It's ok Crystal. I'm feeling alright. I'm just about to pop down to the local newsagents. You're both welcome to come along."

I quickly head back into the living room to pick my cup and then bring it to the kitchen, and getting myself ready to go out. Now I'm ready to go, I pick up my bag, locking the front door behind me, and head down the street towards the newsagents to pick up a few things.

As I pass an old creepy looking house, memories flood back. I recall that it hasn't been lived in since 1981 when the last tenants left suddenly. Rumours have always swirled around the property, suggesting it's haunted by a spirit.

I feel a strange energy as I glance up at the top window, noticing a slight movement in the curtain. Then, a tall ghostly looking woman walks past the upstairs window, vanishing as she reaches the other side.

As I continue walking, I wonder about the reason this lady remains haunting the old house. I make a mental note to look into the history of the place after this weekend, once I've had time with Damian.

I reach the shop and pick up what I need. On my way back, I walk past the abandoned house again, and a strange feeling overcomes me again. It seems there is more than one spirit there who remained

Growing Up With Secrets

earthbound, but also something more negative. Perhaps the male spirit is holding the others back from crossing over, although I do sense his energy is much stronger than theirs.

It feels as though it could well be a family of spirits, with the male spirit keeping them trapped. As I stand there, lost in thought, I glance up to see the male spirit standing at the second floor window staring out the window. The moment he notices me, I get an unsettling feeling, so I begin walking away, continuing towards home.

I look back and see two young children standing at the window with the look of distress, as though they're in need of help. But I can't do anything right now, so I keep walking.

Once I'm a little further down the street, I call on Crystal and mother for assistance. I really need help figuring out what to do about the situation involving these spirits.

"Hello darling, you called for us?" Shaz says

"Hi mum, yes I did. Please can you and Crystal help with checking out the old house?" I replied

"Yes of course we can. Anything particular we are looking for?" Shaz responds

"Curious about the spirits I noticed looking out the windows. Be careful of the male spirit he seems to be rather territorial." I explain

"Don't worry Julia, we will find out for you." Crystal replied

After discussing a plan with them, we eventually find ourselves back at the house, next minute Crystal and mother disappear off to who knows where. I unlock the front door and head straight into the kitchen, putting the kettle on to make myself a cup of coffee. I sit down at the table, take out the newspaper from my bag, and start reading.

Suddenly, out of nowhere, Crystal and mother returned with some new information about the spirits.

"We went back to the house and spoke to the young children," Crystal explains. "The boy is 8 years old, and the girl is 6."

My mother adds, "I spoke to the older lady in the house. Her name is Margaret Springer. She told me that the male spirit is her husband, and he's the one responsible for their deaths. He's the reason they're all stuck here while holding them all hostage."

I pause, deep in thought. Then I reach for my notepad and pen, quickly writing down some brief notes for a rescue plan to help them all cross over into the light. I'll need to research the history of why the husband killed his family in the first place. Tomorrow morning, I'll go to the local library and see if I can uncover any details that might shed light on the situation.

"I ask mother and Crystal if they can go back to the house and ask Margaret for a specific date when they were all killed. This

Growing Up With Secrets

information will be helpful when I look through the files tomorrow at the library."

While waiting, I sit in the living room, and suddenly, I have a premonition. I see a vision of the corridor in the old abandoned house.

The next moment, Margaret's husband walks from one side of the room to the other, looking at me as he passes. I knew instantly that I needed to head there. I quickly got myself ready and then headed out the front door. The house was only about a 10 minute walk down the road.

As I walked, I wondered to myself what could be going on there to trigger this vision. A few minutes later, as I approached the old house, I heard a commotion. *That's not good,* I thought. I quickly ran through the side gate and tried the back door. Luckily, it was unlocked.

I could hear Crystal's voice coming loudly from upstairs, shouting, "Shaz this way quick! He's coming!" They both laughed.

"OMG CRYSTAL WATCH OUT, HE'S BEHIND YOU. THIS WAY QUICKLY!"

Hearing them both laughing, I then heard him shout, "Come back here, you'll regret it ladies! I'll hold you here forever!" I ran down the hallway towards the stairs, thinking, *What the hell have they done to annoy him even more?* Reaching the top of the stairs, I looked over the banister. They both stopped, waved, then ran off, with him chasing them into a room. Suddenly, Crystal appeared next to me saying, "Run this way with us!"

We heard him shout, "WHERE ARE YOU?!" He came out of the room, his face filled with rage. Crystal yelled, "For goodness sake, run! Here he comes, lol!" We split up and ran in different directions down the corridor. I turned around, but he didn't follow me. *Here we go again*, I thought. I ask them to do one thing, and now this whole catastrophe begins.

Looking around the doorway to see where they had gone, it felt like a scene from a *Looney Tunes* sketch, watching those two running from room to room with him in hot pursuit!

Margaret suddenly appeared behind me, saying, "Hello, who are you?"

"Hi my name is Julia. The two nutty women running around are my mother and friend Crystal. I'm here to help cross you all over after I stop the commotion they've caused."

"They didn't start anything. He said, 'Get out,' so your mum said, 'Who are you talking to, silly little man?' That's when the commotion began. He got mad and started chasing them."

Growing Up With Secrets

"Thank goodness for that! Normally, it's those two who start things off by annoying spirits," I said with a chuckle. Margaret laughed and replied, "That's a relief."

"Can you take me to where the children are? I can help cross you all over together."

Margaret replied, "They are in the downstairs living room, hiding."

"Can you head down to get the children ready, and I'll meet you downstairs?"

Margaret disappeared, and I rushed down the stairs to find the living room. I opened the door and saw them all standing by the fireplace, waiting. I could still hear mother and Crystal shouting at each other upstairs, but I focused on the children and Margaret in the living room. They were all very nervous, so I reassured them that everything would be ok. I spoke gently to calm them down and told them to think of positive things. After a couple of minutes, they started to relax.

Then one of them asked, "What is that light in the doorway?" I explained, "It's time to cross over. Don't be afraid. It's a good place for you to find peace." I asked if they all see the light, and they nodded in agreement. They all walked towards the doorway. Looking back, they said, "Thank you," before walking through together.

97

Daniel Cory & Charleine Shepherd

I could still hear the commotion upstairs, so I ran back up the stairs to see them still running around, with the male spirit hot on their heels. I stopped Crystal quickly to tell her to run in different directions from each other, to stop the male spirit from chasing them both.

"Ok Julia," Crystal said. In the next instant, I saw them coming my way, and she turned running towards my mother. Crystal shouted, "KEEP GOING THE SAME WAY!!" Shaz nodded and kept running in the same direction.

I stood there, watching them run in circles, with the male spirit growing angrier by the second. He suddenly stopped in front of me, screaming, "GET OUT OF MY HOUSE, NOWWW!!" I shout to mother and Crystal, "Leave now. I'll meet you both later."

Looking at him, I replied, "Ok, I'm leaving now." I headed back down the stairs, through the back door. The same way I had entered the house

I thought it was best to leave the male spirit in peace. He didn't want to cross over into the light. I was happy that his family had crossed over safely. That's another job done, but I believe the house will remain derelict.

Growing Up With Secrets

CHAPTER 9

Two weeks have now passed since I was at the derelict house on Trifold Drive, helping to cross the family of earthbound spirits into the light, where they eventually found peace. While Crystal and Mumma Shaz kept the male spirit occupied, chasing them around upstairs, I had the time to ensure the family was safely crossed over. Once they had all gone, I made my way back upstairs, noticing them running back and forth noticing it was like a circus in that house for a brief moment.

I still walk past the derelict house from time to time when I pop over to the corner shop for a few bits, and I'll often notice the male spirit watching from the window. I do wonder what will happen next, as it tends to catch me by surprise. But fingers crossed, it won't be for a while, I think to myself, giggling.

Laura will be dropping Damian off to us this Friday for the weekend, and we're so excited to see him. I think I'd better go shopping to get some things ready for when he arrives.

***

It's Friday afternoon, currently waiting for Laura to arrive with Damian. I finish cleaning up some bits around the kitchen and sit at the table to finish doing my crossword puzzle, after a few minutes I hear the door-bell ring. Walking to the front door opening it, there stands Laura with Damian in her arms.

"Hi Julia."

"Hi Laura, how have you been? Please come in, would you like a cup of coffee?"

"I've been doing ok. Yes please, that would be great thank you."

As Laura puts Damian down he runs up towards me, giggling and smiling, shouting, "Nanny!"

"Hello my darling, it's good to see you." I give Damian a kiss and hug, Laura closes the front door behind her. We then head towards the kitchen so I can put the kettle on and make us a hot drink.

"Would you like some orange squash, Damian?" I ask. He looks at me with a cheeky smile and nods excitedly.

"Give me a moment darling, and Nanny will get you a beaker with juice in it."

Laura sits down at the table.

"How have you been, Julia? I guess it's not been the same since we left?"

"It's been bearable. Marcus is doing well at work, although he hasn't taken the situation too well. I've been dealing with the usual

Growing Up With Secrets

supernatural stuff again recently, just a couple of weeks ago at an old house."

"Oh my, what happened?"

"The usual with my mother and Crystal tormenting a male spirit who chased them around this abandoned house just a little way down the street. I managed to cross the family of spirits into the light, then left the property."

"Wow, you do get into some awkward and frustrating situations with spirits!"

"It does, when two spirits start messing around for fun, thinking it's funny!!"

"This is not something I want Damian getting involved with!"

"He was born with a natural gift. You can't stop him from using his gifts Laura, and he has already been involved in it from the very start with my mum and Crystal."

Just as Laura and I are still talking about Damian's involvement with the supernatural, he starts giggling, looking up towards me. The next moment, as I turn around, I'm startled by these two mad women appearing again out of nowhere, pulling funny faces at him.

"How many times have I told you both not to keep appearing like that? You gave me such a jump!!"

Daniel Cory & Charleine Shepherd

"Oh pish posh Julia, get a grip! We aren't that bad! I wanted to see my wonderful great grandson. It's not a crime you know," mother replies.

Crystal is just standing there, giving her attention to Damian, while I have a word with my mother about their appearances. As I turn back around, Laura looks far from impressed, as usual, and she's about to make a comment.

"Julia, this is exactly the situation I'm telling you about. He's only a baby!"

"Hang on a moment Laura. Let me sort out a drink, and we'll have a chat about it."

I get up as the kettle finishes boiling, pouring the hot water into both cups with a drop of milk. Crystal and mother are playing with Damian, keeping him occupied for a moment while I sort out the hot drinks. I give a cup to Laura and sit back down at the table to continue our conversation about the supernatural situations.

Laura still doesn't look too impressed with me. I think to myself she should have more understanding, considering all the situations I've previously dealt with when she was in hospital and Damian was just born. I begin trying to explain again to Laura the importance of these gifts.

Growing Up With Secrets

"Damian has a natural gift, being the firstborn of his generation. It happens to each first born in the family. I'm sorry you don't feel happy with this, but you knew about all this when you were with Marcus!"

"Well, my new partner Gareth doesn't believe in all that rubbish!"

"Laura let me remind you, it has nothing to do with this new guy you're seeing. It's down to Damian to believe or not about his gifts, and he's already playing about with my mum and Crystal"

"How dare you talk to me like that!" She responds

Laura, now in a rage, gets up without saying anything else, storms out of the kitchen, and heads out the front door, slamming it behind her. I look back around to see Crystal, my mum, and Damian all looking at me, shocked by what just happened with Laura.

"Don't worry about what just happened. She needs to understand that the gifts come from your side of the family mum, to each first born child in our family."

"Of course, sweetie. Just ignore her. It looks like she's being influenced by that new partner, Mr. Negativity!"

"Don't worry about it mum. She'll probably go back and tell that muppet now. Laura has changed a lot since she split from Marcus."

***

After slamming the front door of Julia's house, I made my way to the car. Once inside, I took my mobile phone from my handbag and dialled Gareth's number.

Ring, Ring Ring, Ring

Gareth answers: "Hello, darling."

Laura: *Sobbing down the phone*

Gareth: "What's wrong, babe?"

Laura: "I just had a massive argument with Julia over Damian."

Gareth: "Babe, what was it about?"

Laura: "It was about this supernatural stuff and Damian's involvement. I said we didn't want him to be involved in anything she does with it."

Gareth: "Just come home, we can talk about it more then."

Laura: "Ok, I won't be long."

Phone Call Ends

Twenty minutes later, I arrive back home and pull up on the driveway. Getting out of the car, I make my way to the front door. Just as I place the key in the door, Gareth opens it, looking agitated.

"I'm not happy with Julia interfering where it's none of her business," he says. "We need to have a serious chat about this!"

"Let's just get indoors first, I'm not happy with this either," I reply.

Growing Up With Secrets

I walk into the kitchen to get a cold glass of water. "Darling, do you want a drink?"

"No thank you, not right now."

"Ok no problem, I'll be right in."

I then make my way into the living room and sit down on the sofa.

"Laura, can you explain more about what happened at Julia's, regarding this supernatural rubbish involving Damian?"

"Well, it all started when we got there. Julia said her mother and this girl called Crystal showed up. She was talking to them while I just sat there. Julia mentioned that they were interacting and talking to Damian. Damian started to giggle when I couldn't see anything there. That's when I said we weren't happy about that and didn't want Damian around all that stuff."

"What happened after that?"

"Julia said he has a special gift and that it would be Damian's decision what he does. It ended up in a massive argument. I just stormed out in anger!"

"I've had enough of her interfering in things that do not concern her. I'm going to call her up and tell her straight."

Gareth asks me for Julia's phone number as he gets up to use the landline.

105

"The number is 01633721960."

"Thank you babe."

Gareth picks up the phone receiver and dials Julia's number.

Ring, Ring Ring, Ring No answer

He dials again, but the phone continues to ring with no answer. He tries one last time to call Julia's house.

Ring, Ring Ring, Ring

Answer machine: "Hello, you have reached the voicemail of Julia and Marcus Jones. Please leave your name and number at the tone." Beep

"JULIA, THIS IS GARETH! HOW DARE YOU HAVE A GO AT LAURA OVER DAMIAN'S INVOLVEMENT IN YOUR SUPERNATURAL RUBBISH! KEEP YOUR NOSE OUT OF THE DECISIONS WE MAKE FOR HIM, YOU INTERFERING OLD COW. THIS IS YOUR ONLY WARNING!!!"

End of message

Watching Gareth place the receiver back on the phone, he sits down next to me on the sofa.

"Hopefully, now she will get the message about not interfering in our choices for Damian!" he mentions

Growing Up With Secrets

"You hope she does, love. Julia might retaliate to your message. She isn't one to back down easily."

"We'll see after I deal with her myself, babe!"

CHAPTER 10

It's a nice sunny afternoon, while Damian and I are just getting back to the house after spending some time at the park. I was pushing Damian on the swing and then watching him come down the slide. We had a really fun time, seeing him enjoy an afternoon out. As we walked through the hallway, I noticed there was a new message on the answer machine.

We headed into the kitchen to get some lunch sorted out, and then went back into the living room where I sat Damian down in front of the TV to watch cartoons while eating his lunch. Now he is sitting quietly. I went out into the hallway and clicked the play button to listen to the message. It was Gareth leaving a threatening message about the argument I had with Laura regarding Damian's involvement in the supernatural. He's just a twat who seems to throw his weight around. How dare he leave that sort of message! I'm fuming about this, and he will find out when he gets a surprise phone call from me in just a moment.

Picking up the phone receiver, I dialled the home phone number for Laura and Gareth.

Growing Up With Secrets

Ring, Ring Ring, Ring Ring, Ring

Gareth: "Hello, Gareth speaking."

Julia: "Who the hell do you think you are, leaving a threatening message telling me to keep my nose out of decisions that involve my grandson?! He's not related to you!!"

Gareth: "I'm his step father, and I have as much right as you do, Julia."

Julia: "Not while I'm around you don't, you backwards two-faced jalopy!!"

Phone call ends as I slam the receiver down

I just couldn't take the guy anymore. It's so infuriating, it's unreal. Putting the phone down on that twat was the best thing. Now I must calm myself down, as I can't let Damian see me like this. But I hear some familiar voices coming from the living room, with some laughing going on.

The timing couldn't have been better with mother and Crystal showing up to keep an eye on Damian while I'm having a full on war over the phone with a completely backward dodo bird who calls himself a man!

I say to myself, "Three deep breaths, Julia, the guy is not worth getting angry over."

I head back into the living room to see my mother sitting on the floor in front of Damian, but Crystal is nowhere to be seen. Very confusing, as she was here a moment ago.

"JULIAAA HEYYY!" says Crystal.

"OMG, don't do that! How many more times, woman? You're going to give me a heart attack one of these days!"

Crystal just giggles while wandering back towards Damian. I take Damian's plate into the kitchen and make myself a cup of coffee. I put the kettle on and get my cup ready. While I'm standing there waiting for the kettle to boil, I sense the presence of my mother. Just as I turn around, there she is, talking to me about the message on the answer machine.

"What was happening over that phone call you had just now?"

"I had an argument with Laura's new partner, Gareth, who thinks he can tell me he has the right to decide what Damian does."

"He has no right to have any say! Stupid man! Do you want me to go haunt him for you?"

"Hmmm, no mum, it's all ok. I can handle things with that twat!"

"Ok hun, if you change your mind, just let me know, alright?"

"Of course I will mum. Thank you for all the support."

Growing Up With Secrets

The kettle has finished boiling. I pour the hot water into my cup to make a coffee and then go back into the living room to sit in the armchair. Meanwhile, mother and Crystal say they have to go, explaining they'll be back soon.

I do wonder where those two are off to and what they'll get up to now. I put Damian onto his playmat with some toys while I have a quick read through today's paper. Ten minutes had passed, and I hear the front door open, hearing Marcus shout out, "Mum, I'm home!"

"Hello love."

Damian shouts, "DADDY!"

Damian gets up and runs out to see Marcus.

"OMG, hey baby boy!"

Marcus then walks into the living room holding Damian in his arms.

***

"Where are we off to, Shaz?"

"We're going over to Laura's house to annoy that fella of hers!"

"But Julia told us not to worry about it. Should we really go over there?"

Daniel Cory & Charleine Shepherd

"Don't worry. If she finds out, I'll explain everything. That muppet must pay for upsetting my daughter like he did after being rude!"

"What actually happened Shaz?"

"That muppet started saying he has the right to decide what Damian does. It was all because he doesn't believe in the supernatural."

"It's none of his business! We must pay him back for this, regardless of the consequences."

"Exactly, my dear! Now, let's go cause some mayhem. HAHAHA!"

Right now, we're here at Laura's house, and we can start making as much noise as possible by banging on the walls, opening cupboard doors, and slamming them shut.

"Ohhh, this is going to be fun Shaz! Let's start in the kitchen and really spook them both!"

I start by turning the lights on, and Crystal heads over to the sink, turning the water on full blast. The next moment, we see both their heads turn, looking baffled by what has just happened.

"Crystal, come to the fridge. When I open it up, let's start chucking things at them!"

"Oooo, loving this idea Shaz! This will be fun. On your marks, girl!"

"Allow me to open the fridge. Ready Crystal? Hahaha!"

I open the fridge door, and we see Laura's face drop. Crystal grabs a tomato and throws it directly at Gareth's head. We keep grabbing different things and pelting them.

Gareth shouts, "WHAT THE HELL IS GOING ON?!"

Laura replies, "I don't know! Probably something to do with Julia, no doubt."

Gareth says, "How is this even possible? I'm not believing in this supernatural rubbish!"

Laura says, "I'll give Julia a call to come and sort out whoever is here."

Crystal walks up behind them, an egg in each hand. The next moment, she splats the eggs right onto both their heads.

Laura and Gareth both scream. A second later, he yells, "Call Julia, NOW! Something's not right here!"

As we watch Laura run to the house phone to call Julia, we decide to stay just five more minutes while she makes the call. The moment she's done, we'll high-tail it out of here before we get caught!

Daniel Cory & Charleine Shepherd

House phone starts ringing.

Marcus: *"Hello?"*

Laura: *"Marcus, can you put Julia on the phone now?"*

Marcus: *"What do you want mum for?"*

Laura: *"I need to ask her to come over. We've got some issues going on."*

Marcus: *"Ok, hang on a moment."*

I place the phone receiver onto the table for a moment while calling out to mum.

"Mum, Laura's on the phone asking for you."

"Ask her what she wants son, please."

"She mentioned something about having some issues over there. By the sounds of it, this could be supernatural."

"Ok, I'm coming now."

I pick up the phone receiver from the table and hand it to mum.

Julia: *"Hi Laura. What do you want?"*

Laura: *"We've got some strange things going on over here. I believe it could be supernatural."*

I giggle. "Oh no, what's happening?"

Laura: *"Stop giggling, It's not funny! Can you come over or not?"*

Growing Up With Secrets

Julia: *"Yeah, I'll be right over. Hang onto your knickers woman!"*

Laura: *"Hurry, please."*

Julia: *"I'll be there in 20 minutes."*

Laura: *"Ok, thanks. Bye."*

Julia: *"Ta-ta for now."*

Laura hangs up.

I walk back into the living room, laughing to myself, thinking how funny it was hearing Laura panic about whatever's happening.

"What are you laughing at, mum? What's going on?"

"Nothing much son. Sounds like some supernatural stuff happening in their house, so I'm going to see what's going on."

"Ok, please be careful."

"I will son. I'll be back soon. I won't be long."

Picking up my bag, I make my way over to Laura's to see what's been going on. No doubt it's mother and Crystal causing trouble again, despite me telling them not to.

✳✳✳

"Crystal, we have five minutes because Julia is on her way over. Let's make as much mess as possible!"

"Okie dokie!"

We start opening some of the other cupboards and throwing things onto the floor. Crystal chucks a load of flour everywhere, so we both begin making footprints and handprints all over the cupboard doors.

"Crystal, it's time to go, come quickly!"

There's a knock at the front door.

"Babe, can you get the door? That's probably the interfering cow now so she can do some of her voodoo magic!"

"Be civil with Julia, please Gareth. She's come over urgently to help clear up this mess. I'm not happy with her having a go either."

I head towards the front door and open it, seeing Julia standing there.

"Come on in."

As Julia walks through the door, I close it behind her. We head through to the kitchen, where Gareth is cleaning up some of the mess. I see Julia's shocked expression as she takes in the chaos.

Julia says, "Blimey! It looks like a whirlwind tore through here. I don't see anyone here at the moment."

Laura replies, "Are you sure there's no one here? Things just went mad. Stuff was being thrown at us and all over the kitchen!"

Julia responds, "Yes, 100% sure. There are no spirits here."

Laura lets out a sigh of relief. "Thank goodness for that!"

Growing Up With Secrets

***

As I get ready to leave Laura and Gareth's house after dealing with their so called ghost problem, I wonder what on earth had actually happened before I arrived, with Laura in a panic on the phone.

The next moment, mother and Crystal suddenly appear out of nowhere. The shock on my face says it all, I knew straight away that it was those two causing all the commotion and trouble at Laura and Gareth's.

Making my way towards the front door, I open it, step outside, and turn around to say goodbye to Laura before continuing towards the car. As I walk away, I hear the front door close behind me.

"Right, you two maniacs. Show yourselves!"

"You called for us, darling?"

"Yes, I called for you both! What's the big idea throwing things around their kitchen? And don't you dare deny it!"

"We? Nooo, never! Why would it be us, Julia?"

"Oh yeah, right. Like you two wouldn't! Now fess up. It was you and Crystal, wasn't it?"

"Oh, alright fine! It was us. We wanted to teach them both a lesson for what that twat said over the phone to you."

Daniel Cory & Charleine Shepherd

"I thought as much! I just knew it. Well done though, I found it absolutely hilarious!"

I place the key in the ignition and start the car, making my way home to see Marcus and Damian.

As I drive down the road, I take a quick glance in the rear view mirror, only to see that mother and Crystal have already vanished like the wind, as per usual.

While driving, I start thinking about what we're going to have for dinner tonight. Then it occurs to me that Marcus might have already prepared something, given that it's getting close to late afternoon.

Finally, I arrive home, pulling up outside the house. I turn off the engine, step out, and close the car door behind me. Locking up the car, I begin walking up the driveway towards the front door, which suddenly opens, revealing Marcus standing there holding Damian in his arms.

"Look who's back little man, it's Nanny!"

Damian giggles, holding out his arms towards me.

"Come to Nanny, my little darling! Wow, you're getting heavy aren't you?" I chuckle to myself as I walk through the door. Marcus closes it behind me.

Growing Up With Secrets

Suddenly, the delicious aroma of something cooking fills the air. I wonder what it could be.

"What's for dinner son? It smells amazing!"

"It's just chicken curry, nothing fancy. It's my own homemade recipe."

"That's fantastic son! I'm really looking forward to trying it later."

"Won't be long mum. It'll be ready shortly. Just going to check on the rice."

Marcus heads to the kitchen to keep an eye on dinner while I sit in the living room with Damian.

A moment later, something catches my eye seeing someone walking past in the hallway. Quickly, I get up from the armchair to take a look, making sure Damian is distracted by his toys for a moment.

Peering into the hallway, I don't see anyone. Whoever it was must have vanished. Very strange. They didn't stay, yet the energy they left behind feels very distinct. It might be an earthbound spirit, but for now, I'll leave it and see if they show up again.

"Mum dinner will be ready in five minutes."

"Ok son, we'll be right there."

Daniel Cory & Charleine Shepherd

I walk back into the living room and look down at Damian, who gazes up at me with a little smile.

"Come on my little angel,it's time for dinner. Your wonderful daddy has made a homemade meal for us all."

We walk through to the kitchen, and I place Damian in his highchair just as Marcus starts dishing up the food. I prep drinks for everyone.

"Son, what would you like to drink?"

"Can you pour me a glass of Pepsi, please mum?"

I prepare a beaker of apple juice for Damian and pour two glasses of Pepsi, one for Marcus and one for myself.

Marcus places the plates on the table, along with a small bowl for Damian. I take a mouthful of the curry, wow the flavour is incredible.

"Son, this is one of the best curries you've made! Even Damian is enjoying his dinner."

"Thanks mum it's nothing special, but I'm glad you like it."

"You should give yourself more credit son. This was superb!"

As we finish eating, I get up and collect our plates, along with Damian's bowl, and take them to the sink to be washed. Meanwhile, Marcus takes Damian into the living room for ten minutes before taking him upstairs to givehim a bath and then ready for bed.

Growing Up With Secrets

While Marcus is upstairs, I tidy the living room and turn on the TV, hoping to find something worth watching.

I settle into my armchair, but out of the corner of my eye, I see someone walk past the living room door towards the kitchen.

I quickly get up to check again, when I look no one is there.

Turning back, I return to my armchair, only for Crystal and my mother to appear out of nowhere.

I talk with them both for a few minutes before Marcus comes back downstairs after putting Damian to bed.

Before they leave, I ask them to keep an eye out for the spirit that keeps appearing and disappearing in the hallway.

CHAPTER 11

Waking up, I realise morning has arrived already. I wonder where the hours have gone, as the night seems to have passed so quickly. Glancing at the clock on my bedside cabinet, I see it's only 7:30 am.

Lying in bed, I decide to have an extra ten minutes before getting up to make a cup of coffee. Eventually, I make my way out of the bedroom and into the hallway, calling out to Marcus.

"Son, it's time to get up. Can you get Damian before you come downstairs, please? I'm going to make some coffee."

Heading down the stairs, I walk into the kitchen, fill the kettle up with water, and switch it on to boil. I take out the cups, preparing everything. I'll get Damian's milk ready for him when he comes down with Marcus.

I hear movement in the hallway, but as I glance towards the doorway, I see the spirit standing there just staring at me. Then, in an instant, it vanishes again. I still don't understand who this could be, but hopefully, when mother and Crystal arrive, they'll shed some light on it.

A moment later, Marcus comes downstairs with Damian in his arms, both of them laughing as they walk into the kitchen.

Growing Up With Secrets

I smile at Damian. "What would you like for breakfast, my darling?"

"Porridge Nan Nan."

"Nan Nan will put some chopped bananas on top too."

Placing a small bowl of porridge with chopped bananas in front of him, Damian picks up his spoon and starts eating. I glance over at Marcus, who is sipping his morning coffee while reading the newspaper.

"Would you like anything for breakfast while I'm making something for myself, son?"

"Yes please mum. Could you do me two slices of toast with butter?"

"Of course I can. It'll be ready in just a moment."

"Thanks mum."

I pop two slices of bread into the toaster. While they're cooking, I prepare some porridge and fruit for myself. Just as I place my bowl on the table, I notice something behind Marcus when Crystal and my mother appear.

Damian giggles, looking at Crystal as she pulls funny faces at him. The expression on Marcus's face, however, tells a different story as he looks completely baffled by what Damian is laughing at. A moment later, he turns to me.

"Mum, what is he laughing at?"

"It's just your Nan coming to say hi. Crystal is here too, she's pulling funny faces at Damian to make him laugh!"

"Ohhhh. Hey Nan! How are you?"

"Julia, tell Marcus I'm doing alright, and I hope he's doing ok too."

"Nan says she's doing alright son, and she asks how you are."

"I'm doing good, thanks Nan. Just been busy with little man and work."

"Julia, we have some information about the female spirit that's been appearing to you recently."

"Ok. Give me about twenty minutes to finish my breakfast and coffee, then we can sit down and talk."

"No problem darling. Just call for me and Crystal when you're ready." As they both vanish

Finishing off my porridge and coffee, I get up and clear the table, placing everything in the sink ready to be washed. Marcus picks Damian up and takes him back upstairs for a quick bath and to get him dressed.

Growing Up With Secrets

I quickly wash up the cups, plate, and bowls, leaving them on the draining board before reaching a towel to dry them and putting them away in the cupboards.

Calling out to mum and Crystal, I let them know I'm ready to sit down and discuss this female earthbound spirit. I make my way into the living room and settle into my armchair, waiting for both to appear as they always do.

"JULIAAAA, WE'RE COMING FOR YOU!!!"

"Oh, shut up and get your butts in this living room so we can talk about this earthbound lady! It's too early for your playground antics this morning."

"Ok, ok we're here! So, where do we start?"

"The beginning might help. I've got my notepad ready to write down whatever information you two clowns have gathered for me!"

"Alright, here we go…"

Notes Regarding the Earthbound Female Spirit:

- ***Name: Diane Blakemore***

- ***Born: 21st November 1987 (Aged 36)***

- ***Cause of death: Severe blood loss during childbirth due to a major haemorhage. She gave birth to a healthy baby girl but sadly passed away ten minutes later.***

- *Her baby girl was born on the same day as Damian and was later placed in the care of her aunt, Sally Blakemore, as the father was not present at the birth. The hospital staff were later informed that he wanted nothing to do with his newborn daughter.*

- *Diane has been wandering around the hospital, earthbound, since the day she died in the delivery room. She sensed your energy after you attended the memorial service in the hospital chapel but was unable to find you quickly enough while still adjusting to the spirit world.*

"Thank you for all this information. It will help us cross Diane into the light, but in the meantime, see if you can track her down while I search for information on her sister, Sally."

"No problem, leave that to us, Julia. We'll be back soon. If you need us, just holler!"

I laugh to myself when Crystal says, "Just holler." Now that I have all the information I need, later I can pop over to the local library to see if there are any available records for Sally Blakemore. With those two troublemakers vanishing to who knows where, I can now head upstairs for a quick wash and get dressed, ready to start the day.

Growing Up With Secrets

As I reach the top of the stairs, I hear Marcus making funny voices while dressing Damian. Smiling, I head into my room, gather my clothes, and go to the bathroom.

Emerging from the bathroom, I mention to Marcus about us all going on a family day out to Folly Farm Adventure Park and Zoo. They have a variety of activities for children, including a small petting zone where visitors can see the animals up close.

"That sounds like great fun mum! Damian will definitely enjoy himself. What time are we leaving?"

"As soon as we're already son."

"We're both ready mum. I'll meet you downstairs with little man."

"Ok love. Give me two minutes, and I'll be down."

Marcus heads downstairs with Damian while I quickly search my room for the Polaroid camera. Thinking about where on earth I last placed it, I suddenly remember and open the drawer—there it is. Picking it up out the draw, I make my way back downstairs, walking into the living room to pick up my bag from beside the armchair. I slip the camera inside my bag.

Calling out to Marcus, I ask, "Are you ready son?"

"Yeah, we're ready mum."

We all head out the front door. Marcus takes Damian to the car and straps him into his car seat. I lock up the house, double checking the front door, then make my way to the passenger side of the car.

"Right, everything's locked up, and we're good to go son."

"Okie dokie mum. Here we go!"

Marcus pulls off the driveway, and we start our journey to the zoo. I find myself thinking about what animals we'll see first and decide to ask Damian. Turning to look into the backseat, I suddenly notice mother and Crystal appearing out of nowhere silently, without me even sensing their energy. They both just sit there smiling at me while Damian looks out the window.

Then, as quickly as they appeared, the two of them wave and vanish, as if they were never there. For a brief moment, I think to myself, here we go again, another round of the 'morning car appearance madness show.'

Shaking it off, I refocus on Damian.

"Are you going to tell Nanny which animal you'd like to see first at the zoo?"

"Want to see the stripy tigers, Nanny!"

"We'll head straight to Tiger Land when we arrive."

Growing Up With Secrets

Damian hugs his cuddly toy, giggling, and even Marcus joins in laughing with us, just as we arrive at the zoo and park up

We head through to the main complex of the zoo after paying at reception for our ticket. It's a beautiful sunny day, and when we reach the tiger enclosure, we see two white tigers playing in a pool that the zookeepers have filled for them. We watch them splashing around for a while before moving on to the next enclosure, where we spot the otter family. Some are floating in the water, while others basking on the rocks, soaking up the sun.

We stand there for a while, watching the otters attempt to crack open the shells they've been given. Damian sits on Marcus's shoulders, laughing as the otters struggle to get to their food.

Glancing to my right, I notice a young lady standing nearby, completely soaked and looking very unhappy. I wonder if she's ok and I pause for a moment, debating whether to approach her. Just as I decide to walk over, I see someone walk straight through her. My breath catches realising she's an earthbound spirit.

I can't believe I didn't pick up on the signs sooner. Quickly tapping Marcus on the shoulder, I tell him, "I'm just popping to the bathroom."

By the time I turn back around, the girl has vanished from where she was standing. Without wasting time, I make my way to the bathroom.

Daniel Cory & Charleine Shepherd

Once inside, I close the cubicle door and whisper, "Pssst! Mother, Crystal, get your butts here now. It's urgent!"

Almost immediately, I hear sniggering from the cubicles on either side of me. Standing there, I wonder what on earth these people find so funny.

Then suddenly without warning.

"Boo! We're here!"

Startled, I lose my balance and fall straight back onto the toilet seat. Looking up I see those two lunatics peering over at me from either side of the cubicle walls.

"What the hell do you two think you're playing at? Seriously! This happens far too often. Now, can I get your help, or is that too much to ask?"

"Sorry darling, we were only joking! Now what do you need our help with?"

"Yeah come on, tell us Julia! Pleeease?"

"Well, if you'd calm yourselves woman, I'll tell you."

"Ohh, sorry Julia."

"Right, I need you to look around the zoo and see if you can find any trace of a young lady. She looks about 18 years old, has wet clothes, and is very angry."

Growing Up With Secrets

"Yep, leave it to us love. We'll be back as soon as we have more information."

"Thank you both. See you later."

Now that's one problem sorted. Sending those two nutters off on a task gives me a moment of peace. I focus on cleaning myself up and head back to the boys before Marcus starts wondering where I've disappeared to.

When I return, they're still in the same spot watching the otters. I tap Marcus on the shoulder.

"Are you ready to go see what other animals they have here?"

"Yes mm. Ready when you are."

We make our way over to the monkeys, who are all swinging around on the ropes and chasing each other on the ground. All we can hear is Damian giggling loudly at their antics. As we stand there, one of the zookeepers enters the enclosure with a box of fruit and begins throwing it around for the monkeys, each one grabbing whatever pieces they can. Meanwhile, Marcus reads from the information board in front of him, explaining what monkeys do in the wild.

Glancing at the zoo leaflet I check what shows are taking place today. There's a dolphin show in the aquarium stadium at 11:00 am. That sounds like a lovely idea to watch the dolphins perform after getting a cup of tea and something to eat. I mention it to Marcus to see what he thinks.

"Son, shall we get a quick cup of tea and a bite to eat, then head over for the morning dolphin show?"

"Let's do that mum. Sounds like a perfect idea."

We make our way over to the café and find a table to sit at while we browse the menu.

"What would you like to eat and drink?" I ask Marcus.

"I'll have a ham salad sandwich with a black coffee. Let's get Damian a small portion of chips with a carton of juice. What about you mum?"

"I'll have the cheese and ham salad sandwich with a glass of Coke, please son. Here's £10 before you head over to pay."

"Thanks mum. I'll be back in a moment."

While Marcus goes to order the food and drinks, I glance down at Damian, who is staring intently out of the window. His usual giggles are gone, replaced by a look of deep focus. Curious, I turn to see what has caught his attention.

Outside the café, I spot the drowned lady again. She's standing there pointing at us with a confused expression, her head tilted to the

Growing Up With Secrets

right. The next moment she suddenly runs off, and then I hear someone shout that sounds like Crystal's voice.

"OIIIIIII! GET BACK HERE YOU!"

Crystal sprints past chasing after the girl, while mother follows behind, running like an old tart in heels.

Five minutes later, the lady comes dashing back past the café window, still being pursued by Crystal, who is still screaming at her. Mother clearly exhausted, pauses for a quick breather before continuing the chase even though it's confusing to watch.

Damian and I burst into giggles, watching the ridiculous scene unfold outside just as Marcus returns to the table with our drinks.

"What are you two laughing at so much?"

"Oh son. I asked Nan and Crystal to help with a situation involving a young lady in spirit. They went off to look for her, and now they're chasing her past the café window like some comedy show!"

"That would have been amazing to see! I wish I had the gift like you both do."

"You might have it son. There could be a blockage in your spiritual centers. We'll figure it out though."

"I hope so mum. Then I'd be like you being able to help people when they need it, and I could even interact with Nan and Crystal."

The waitress arrives with our food, placing it on the table.

"Is there anything else I can get for you?"

"Not at the moment, thank you for bringing this over."

"You're very welcome."

Marcus squeezes some tomato sauce onto Damian's chips and pops the straw into his juice carton. We all start eating, but my mind is already planning what else we'll do today at the zoo. Hopefully, I'll also get more information about the spirit lady once mother and Crystal stop playing chase around the place.

I glance at Marcus and notice he looks deep in thought while eating. I wonder if it has to do with our conversation about his spiritual gifts just before the waitress arrived.

"Son, is everything ok? You look like you're lost in thought."

"Yes, sorry mum. I'm alright, just thinking about stuff. Nothing important."

"If you ever want to talk about anything, I'm always here to listen."

"Thanks mum."

"You're welcome love. We'll head over to the dolphin show in about twenty minutes once we've finished eating."

"There's still plenty of time as we still have half hour before the show starts."

Growing Up With Secrets

At that moment, mother appears beside me with more information about the drowned lady. Surprisingly, Crystal is nowhere to be seen. That's unusual.

"Julia, I have some more information regarding the lady who drowned. And don't ask where Crystal has gone because I have no idea."

"What did you find out mum?"

"The girl told us she was 19 years old and died in an accident while working in the orca whale marine pool area. She remembers slipping into the water, and the orca drowned her. The next moment, she was in spirit watching as people pulled her body out of the pool."

"Thanks mum. That's really helpful. It gives me something to research later when we get home. Did she mention her name at all?"

"Her name was Katie. That was all she said before vanishing."

"That'll help as it gives me a lead for my search later."

"No problem love. I'll go find Crystal and see where she's disappeared to. I'll catch up with you later."

"Thanks mum. Try not to get into too much mischief!"

"Mischief? Us? Never!"

Mother then vanishes to search for Crystal. Meanwhile, Marcus is cleaning Damian up now they have both finished their food, and I quickly writing down all the information mother has provided before I forget any details. I manage to finish off the last part of my sandwich and glance up at the clock, noticing it's nearly time for the dolphin show to begin.

Marcus turns to me and asks, "Are you ready to go mum?"

"Yes, I'm ready. Let's start making our way to the dolphin show centre son."

"I'll get Damian into his pushchair mum."

"Ok son."

We gather our belongings and leave the café, strolling along the pathway towards the dolphin show centre, which is only a five-minute walk away. Something in the air feels off where it's a strange energy that I can't quite place my thoughts on it, but it does seem connected to something significant.

As we approach the dolphin centre, I place my hand on a fence, and suddenly a psychic vision is triggered. In an instant, I find myself standing next to the orca whale pool. I see Katie near the edge while feeding the orca whale fish from a bucket. She turns to grab another bucket of fresh fish but slips, falling into the water. The orca immediately bites on to her leg dragging her beneath the water refusing to let go as she struggles desperately for air. Within minutes she suffocates from being under underwater for too long.

Growing Up With Secrets

A crowd of people gather at the gates, screaming for staff to help, but by the time they reach the pool it was too late. Her lifeless body floats on the surface after the orca whale finally releases its grip. Two staff members pull her from the water and attempt CPR, but their efforts are in vain.

Suddenly, the vision ends, and I find myself back in reality with Marcus speaking to me.

"Mum, are you ok? Did you have a psychic vision?"

"Yes I did son. I saw everything that happened to this young lady Katie and saw how she died here."

"Is that the spirit you asked Nan and Crystal to find?"

"It was indeed. What a tragic accident. When I do my research later hopefully it should reveal more information."

"What exactly happened to her mum?"

"It's best I don't say anything for now. Let's wait until we're back home."

"Ok. The show starts in ten minutes. We should go buy our tickets and then find some seats."

"I agree son. Let's go."

Daniel Cory & Charleine Shepherd

The doors to the dolphin centre are already open, so we walk straight in and head to the ticket counter. I notice an amazing gift shop that we can explore after the show.

The ticket attendant greets us. "Hello, how can I help?"

"Hi, could we have two adult and one child tickets for the dolphin show please?"

"Certainly. Let me just enter that into the system. That will be £10 please."

"I'll pay for this one mum."

"Thank you."

The attendant hands Marcus our tickets. "Enjoy the show!"

We proceed through the doors into the seating area, which, despite being packed with people, still has plenty of available seats. We take a spot right at the front ensuring a great view of the show. After reaching the front row of vacant seats, Marcus unclips the pushchair straps and picking Damian up. We take a seat with Damian sitting happily on Marcus's lap giggling away with excitement.

The show is just beginning when I glance over and to my surprise, I spot mother and Crystal appearing out of nowhere, performing some ridiculous dance around the entertainers. I think to myself, *Oh, good heavens, they're at it again!*

Growing Up With Secrets

Damian is thoroughly enjoying himself, laughing as the dolphins leap gracefully out of the water, while my mother and Crystal continue their antics in the background.

After a few moments, Marcus leans over to me. "Mum, this is a brilliant show so far."

"It sure is son."

I can't help but think to myself that he hasn't noticed the full extent of what's going on. Honestly, it's quite funny even though it's mildly embarrassing. But it all depends on what mother and Crystal decide to do next is the question.

Suddenly, a short scream erupts from the right hand side near the exit. I turn my head and see the same lady we've been trying to learn more about. She shouts, "YOU SUCK!!!"

That certainly gets mother and Crystal's attention without hesitation. They immediately stop dancing and turn their heads fast in the young lady's direction.

"EXCUSE ME! WHO DO YOU THINK YOU ARE?" Crystal bellows.

Without hesitation, she bolts towards the lady, but before she manages to reach her, I see the lady vanish. Predictably, mother follows suit. Marcus and I exchange glances, knowing exactly what this means, and I also think *here we go again.*

I quickly inform Marcus that I'll step outside for a moment and make my way through the main lobby to the entrance. Just as I step outside, I catch sight of the lady sprinting past at an incredible speed, with Crystal hot on her heels and mother lagging behind at a slower pace.

At this point, I decide its best not to get involved. *Nope, not entertaining this nonsense.*

A moment later, they all run past in the opposite direction. Shaking my head, I turn back towards the dolphin show and re-enter the seating area just in time for the final part.

The last part of the performance features entertainers dressed as pirates, and Damian is absolutely excited while watching the dolphins leap in and out of the water. The lead entertainer thanks the audience, and everyone erupts into cheers and applause. As the performers exit, guests begin to stand and make their way towards the main lobby.

"Mum, that was a brilliant show! You missed some of the dolphins' best tricks."

"Sorry son. Nan and Crystal got distracted and started chasing after that young lady again. It was chaos."

"So that's why you stepped out for a moment?"

Growing Up With Secrets

"Yep, that's exactly why."

"Are we heading home now?"

"Yes, I think it's time. Even Damian is yawning, but it's been a great day."

"Before we go, I want to stop in the gift shop and get Damian a small cuddly toy."

"Ok son, that's fine. Perhaps a tiger toy for him?"

"I was thinking of a dolphin, but he can have both."

We walk towards the gift shop entrance and pick up a cuddly tiger and dolphin for Damian, noticing he has already dozed off in his pushchair. I take them to the cashier and pay for both before we head towards the zoo exit.

As we leave, I glance around and unsurprisingly see the young lady still being chased by Crystal and my mother, darting from one area to the next.

They must be exhausted by now, I think to myself.

Smiling, I turn away and continue walking with Marcus and Damian as we are making our way out of the zoo after a fantastic family day out.

Daniel Cory & Charleine Shepherd

CHAPTER 12

Waking up to find out it's morning already, I wonder where those hours have gone as the night has passed by so fast. I take a look at the clock on my bedside cabinet, realising it's only 7:30 am.

Lying in bed, I decide to have an extra 10 minutes before getting up to head downstairs to make a cup of coffee. I get out of bed making my way out of the bedroom to the hallway, giving a shout to Marcus.

"Son, it's time to get up. Can you get Damian before you come downstairs, please? I'm going to make some coffee."

After coming down the stairs, I walk into the kitchen and fill the kettle up, switching it on to boil the water and getting the cups out ready. I'll get Damian's milk ready for him when he comes down with Marcus.

I hear movement in the hallway, but when I look round the doorway, noticing a spirit is standing there, staring at me. Then it vanishes again. I still don't understand who this might be, hopefully mother and Crystal will be able to shed some light on this when they get here.

The next moment, Marcus comes down the stairs with Damian in his arms, then walks into the kitchen while both of them laugh away. I ask Damian what he would like for breakfast.

142

Growing Up With Secrets

"What would you like for breakfast, my darling?"

"Porridge, peas nan nan

"Nan-Nan will put some chopped bananas on top too."

Placing the small bowl of porridge with chopped bananas in front of Damian, he picks up the spoon and starts eating it. I look over to see Marcus sipping his morning coffee while reading the newspaper.

"Would you like anything for breakfast while I'm up making myself something, son?"

"Yes please mum. Could you do me two slices of toast with butter?"

"Of course I can. It will be with you in just a moment son."

"Thanks Mum."

Placing two slices of bread into the toaster, I decide that while that is cooking, I'll make myself some porridge with fruit. Just as I place my bowl onto the table, I look over behind Marcus, and the next minute Crystal and mother appear.

Damian giggles away while looking at Crystal, who is pulling funny faces at him. Meanwhile, the look on Marcus's face tells a different story as he looks baffled by what Damian is giggling at. Then, the next moment, he looks directly at me and says,

"Mum, what is he laughing at?"

143

Daniel Cory & Charleine Shepherd

"It's just your Nan coming to say hi. Crystal is here too, pulling funny faces at Damian to make him laugh!"

"Ohhhh. Hey nan, how are you?"

"Julia tell Marcus that I'm doing alright, and I hope you are doing ok too."

"Nan said she is doing alright son, and she asks how you are."

"I'm doing good thanks nan, just been busy with little man and work."

"Julia, we have some information regarding the female spirit that is currently earthbound. The one who has been appearing to you most recently."

"Ok, give me about 20 minutes to have my breakfast and cup of coffee, then we can sit down to talk."

"No problem darling. Just shout for me and Crystal when you're ready."

After finishing my porridge and coffee, I get up and collect everything, placing it in the sink ready to be washed. Marcus picks Damian up and takes him upstairs to give him a quick bath and get him dressed.

Growing Up With Secrets

I quickly wash up the cups, plates, and bowls, placing them on the draining board. Then I pick up the towel, dry everything, and put them away in the cupboards.

I call out to mum and Crystal, letting them know I'm ready to sit down and talk about this female earthbound spirit. Making my way into the living room, I sit in my armchair and wait for mother and Crystal to appear like they always do.

"JULIAAAA, WE'RE COMING FOR YOU!!!"

"Oh shut up and get your butts in this living room so we can talk about this earthbound lady. It's too early for your playground antics this morning."

"Ok, we're here. So, where do we start?"

"The beginning might help. I have my notepad ready to write down the information you two clowns have gathered for me!"

"Ok, here we go."

Notes regarding the earthbound female spirit:

- **Name:** Diane Blakemore

- **Born:** 21st November 1987 (Aged 36 years)

- **Cause of Death:** Severe blood loss during childbirth due to a major haemorrhage. She gave birth to a healthy baby girl, but Diane sadly passed away 10 minutes later.

- **Her baby girl:** Born on the same day as Damian. Later released into the care of her aunt, Sally Blakemore, as the father was not present at the birth. The hospital staff were later informed that he did not want anything to do with his newborn daughter.

- **Spirit Activity:** She has been wandering the hospital, earthbound, since the day she died in the delivery room. She later sensed your energy after you attended the memorial service in the hospital chapel but was unable to find you quickly enough, as she was still new to the spirit world.

"Thank you for all this information. It will help us to cross Diane into the light, but in the meantime, see if you can track her down while I search for information on her sister Sally."

"Ok no problem. Leave that to us Julia. We'll be back soon. If you need us, just holla!"

I just laugh to myself when Crystal says, "Just holla." Now that all the information has been provided, I can pop over to the local library to see if there is anything available regarding Sally Blakemore's address. With those two troublemakers doing their usual vanishing act to goodness knows where, I can now head upstairs to have a quick wash and get dressed, ready to start the day.

Growing Up With Secrets

Just as I reach the top of the stairs, I hear Marcus making funny voices to Damian while getting him dressed. I head into my room to gather my clothes and then go to the bathroom. Coming out, I mention to Marcus about us all going for a family day out to Folly Farm Adventure Park and Zoo. They have a variety of different activities for children, including a small petting zone where visitors can see the animals up close.

"That sounds like great fun mum Damian will certainly enjoy himself, no doubt. What time are we leaving?"

"As soon as we're all ready son."

"We're both ready mum. I'll meet you downstairs with little man."

"Ok love. Give me two minutes, and I'll be down."

Marcus starts heading downstairs with Damian while I quickly hunt around my room for the Polaroid camera, trying to remember where on earth I last placed it. The next moment, the thought comes to me, and I open the drawer to notice there it is! Quickly picking it up, I make my way downstairs, walk into the living room, and pick up my bag from the side of my chair. I put the camera into my bag and call out to Marcus.

"Are you ready son?"

"Yeah, we're ready mum."

We all make our way out the front door. Marcus takes Damian to the car, opens the back door, and puts him into the car seat. I lock up the house, making sure the front door is double-locked before heading to the car and getting into the passenger side.

"Right, that's everything locked up, and we're good to go son."

"Okie dokie mum, here we go!"

Marcus pulls the car off the driveway, and we make our way up the road to begin our day trip to the zoo. I start thinking about which animals we'll see first and then consider asking Damian which animal he'd like to see first. Looking around into the back, I suddenly notice that mother and Crystal have appeared silently, without me even sensing their energy. They both just sit there smiling at me, while Damian looks out of the car window.

The next moment, these two nutters decide to wave and then vanish, as if they were never sitting there in the first place. Thinking about this for a brief moment, I conclude it's just another episode of the morning car appearance madness show.

I turn my attention back to Damian.

"Are you going to tell Nanny what animal you'd like to see first at the zoo?"

"Want to see the stripy tigers, Nanny!"

Growing Up With Secrets

"We'll head straight to Tiger Land when we arrive."

Damian hugs his cuddly toy while giggling away at me, and even Marcus starts laughing along with us.

It's a nice warm sunny day, and the tigers are playing in the pool that the zookeepers have filled up for them. There are two white tigers splashing around. After watching them for a while, we decide to move across to the next enclosure to spot where the otter family is hiding. Some are floating in the water, while others are sunbathing on the side.

We stand there for a while, watching the otters in the water trying to crack open the shells they have been given. Damian sits on Marcus's shoulders, laughing away as the otters continue struggling to open the shells.

I look over to my right and notice a young woman standing there soaking wet and looking very unhappy. I briefly wonder where her family could be. I wait for a moment before deciding to walk over to her, but the next thing I see is someone walking straight through her. That immediately tells me she is an earthbound spirit.

Not sure why I didn't spot the signs sooner, I quickly tap Marcus on the shoulder to let him know I'm popping off to the bathroom. When I turn back around, the young woman has vanished from the spot where she was standing. With that, I make my way to the bathroom.

149

Daniel Cory & Charleine Shepherd

Once inside the bathroom, I decide to call the two nutters. I'll wait until I'm in a cubicle Before calling for them.

"Pssst! Mother, Crystal get your butts here now! It's urgent!"

I suddenly hear sniggering coming from the right and left cubicles. I stand there, wondering what on earth these people are laughing at.

"Boo! We're here!"

Startled, I fall straight back onto the toilet—without realising the lid was up! Looking up, I see the two loonies peering over at me from either side of the cubicles.

"What the hell do you two think you're playing at? Seriously! This happens far too often. Now, I need your help if you don't mind!"

"Sorry darling, we were only joking about. Now, what do you need our help with?"

"Yeah come on, tell us Julia, pleeease!"

"Well, if you would calm yourself woman, I'll tell you."

"Ohh sorry Julia."

"Please can you look around the zoo to find any trace of a young woman? She looks about nineteen years old, she was wearing wet clothes, and is very angry."

"Yep, leave it to us love. We'll come back as soon as we have more information."

Growing Up With Secrets

"Thank you both. See you later."

Now that's one thing sorted, getting rid of those two nutters for a while. I can now focus on getting myself cleaned up and return to the boys before they start wondering where I am.

The boys are still in the same area where I left them, watching the otters playing in the water and sunbathing. I tap Marcus on the shoulder and ask, "Are you ready to go see what other animals they have here?"

"Yes mum, ready when you are."

We make our way over to the monkeys. They are all swinging around on the ropes and chasing each other on the ground. All we hear is Damian giggling loudly at the monkeys playing around. As we stand there, one of the zookeepers walks into the enclosure with a box of fruit. He starts throwing pieces to the monkeys, and each one grabs whatever it can get hold of. Meanwhile, Marcus reads aloud from the information board in front of him, explaining what monkeys do in the wild.

I check the zoo leaflet for today's scheduled shows. There's a dolphin show in the aquarium stadium starting at 11:00 am. That sounds like a nice idea after getting a cup of tea and something to eat. I mention it to Marcus to see what he thinks.

"Son, shall we head over to get a quick cup of tea and a bite to eat? Then we can go to the morning dolphin show."

"Let's do that mum. Sounds like a perfect idea."

We make our way over to the café and find a table to sit at while looking at the menu. I ask Marcus, "What would you like to eat and drink?"

"I'm going to have a ham salad sandwich with a black coffee. Let's get Damian a small portion of chips with a carton of juice. What are you having mum?"

"I'll have the cheese and ham salad sandwich with a glass of Coke, please son. Just before you go to pay, here's £10."

"Thanks mum. I'll be back in a moment."

While Marcus heads over to pay for the food and drinks, I glance down at Damian, who is staring at something outside the window. He's not smiling or giggling although his attention is completely fixed on something.

Turning to look out the window, I spot the drowned lady again. She stands there pointing at us with a confused expression, her head tilted to the right. The next moment, she runs off, and then I hear the two nutters screaming after her.

"OIIIIIII! GET BACK HERE YOU!!!"

Growing Up With Secrets

Crystal sprints past after the woman, with mother somewhat running behind like an old tart in heels. Five minutes later, the lady runs back past, followed by Crystal still screaming at her, while mother stops for a quick breather before continuing after them, realising she shouldn't be out of breath since she's in spirit.

Damian and I can't help but giggle as we watch this scene unfold outside the café window. Just then, Marcus arrives back at the table with our drinks.

"What are you two laughing at so much?"

"Ohhh son, I asked Nan and Crystal to help me with a situation involving a young lady. They went off to find her, and the next thing I see, they're chasing after her outside the café window like some kind of comedy show!"

"It would be so good to have seen it. I don't have the gifts like you both do."

"You might have the gift son, but there could be a blockage in your spiritual energy centre's. We'll figure it out."

"I hope so mum. Then I'd be like you, so I could help you and others when they need it. Also having the chance to interact with nan and Crystal."

Daniel Cory & Charleine Shepherd

The waitress comes over with our food on a tray, placing it down on the table.

"Is there anything else I can get for you?"

"Not at the moment. Thank you for bringing this over."

"You're very welcome."

Marcus squeezes tomato sauce onto Damian's chips and puts the straw into his juice carton. We all start eating, while my mind drifts to what else might happen today at the zoo. Hopefully, mother and Crystal will stop playing chase long enough to give me more information about this spirit roaming around the zoo.

I glance at Marcus and notice he looks deep in thought while eating. I wonder if it's because of what we were discussing about his spiritual gifts just before the waitress brought our food.

"Son, is everything ok? You look very deep in thought."

"Yes, sorry mum. I'm alright just thinking about stuff. Nothing important."

"If you ever want to talk about anything, I'm always happy to listen son."

"Thanks mum."

"You're welcome son. We'll head over to the dolphin show in twenty minutes once we've finished eating."

Growing Up With Secrets

"Still plenty of time. We have another half an hour before the show starts

The next minute, mother turns up with more information about the drowned ghost lady. Even I am shocked to see that Crystal has not appeared beside her. I begin to wonder what is going on.

"Julia, I have some more information regarding this lady who drowned. Don't ask where Crystal has gotten to because I have no idea."

"What information do you have mum?"

"The young lady told us she was 19 years old and had died in an accident while working in the orca whale marine pool. She remembers slipping into the pool, and the orca whale drowned her. The next moment, she was in spirit watching the zoo employees dragged her body out of the water."

"Thanks mum, that is really helpful. It gives me something to research later at home. Did she mention her name at all?"

"Her name was Katie. That was all she said before vanishing."

"That will help a lot. It gives me something to search when looking into this later

"No problem, Julia. I'll go find Crystal to see where she has gotten to. I'll catch up with you later."

"OK, thanks Mum. Keep out of mischief!"

"Us? Mischief? Never!!"

Mother then vanishes to go in search of where Crystal is. Marcus is cleaning Damian up now that they have both finished their food. I quickly write down all the information mother has provided before I forget anything. I manage to finish off the last part of my sandwich and glance up at the clock, seeing that it is nearly time for the dolphin show to begin.

Marcus then asks me, "Are you ready to go mum?"

"Yes, I'm ready. Let's start getting ready to make our way to the dolphin show centre son."

"I'll sort Damian out into his pushchair mum."

"Ok son, no problem at all."

We gather our things and leave the café, walking across the pathway towards the dolphin show centre, which is only a five-minute walk away. Something in the air feels strange with the energy and it doesn't feel right to me. This sensation is odd, like it has a connection to something.

The next moment, as we approach the dolphin centre, I touch a fence, and it triggers a psychic vision. Suddenly, I find myself standing next to the orca whale pool. I see Katie standing near the edge, feeding

Growing Up With Secrets

the orca whale some fish. She turns around to get the other bucket of fresh fish but suddenly slips, falling into the water.

The orca whale grabs hold of Katie by her lower leg, dragging her down under the water, refusing to let go. She struggles to break free and swim up to get some air, but after a few minutes, she suffocates underwater. A crowd of people gathers at the gates, screaming for staff to help Katie, but by the time they reach the pool, it was too late. Her body floats lifeless in the water after the orca whale finally releases its grip. Two staff members pull her out of the water and attempt CPR, but they have no luck in resuscitating her.

The vision ends suddenly, and I find myself back in reality with Marcus speaking to me.

"Mum, are you alright? Did you have a psychic vision?"

"Yes, I did son. I saw everything that happened to this young lady, who died here."

"Was that the spirit you asked nan and Crystal to find?"

"It was indeed. What a tragic accident it was for this poor girl. When I do my research later, it should come up."

"What happened to her mum?"

"Best I don't say anything for now. Let's wait until we've finished our day out and were back home."

157

"Ok. The show will be starting in ten minutes. We'd best get ourselves some seats."

"I agree son. Let's go."

The door to the dolphin centre is already open, so we walk straight through towards the ticket counter. I notice they have an amazing gift shop to look at when we come out of the show.

The ticket person greets us. "Hello, how can I help?"

"Hi, could we have two adult and one child tickets for the dolphin show, please?"

"Certainly. Let me just put that in the system. The total will be £10, please."

"I'll pay for this one mum."

"Thank you, here are your tickets. Enjoy the show!"

Marcus takes the tickets for us all, and we walk through the doors to the seating area. Despite how packed it is, there is plenty of space. We take seats right at the front, ensuring a good view of the show, especially for Damianto watch the dolphins up close while he sits on Marcus's lap giggling with excitement.

The show begins, and just as I glance over, mother and Crystal decide to appear doing some heinous dance around the entertainers. I think to myself, *Oh, good heavens, they are at it again!*

Growing Up With Secrets

Damian giggles away as he watches the dolphins start their performance, with my mother and Crystal adding their own act in between. After a moment, Marcus turns to me.

"Mum, this is a brilliant show so far."

"It sure is son."

I think silently to myself, he hasn't even seen the whole of what is going on. How embarrassing! These two muppets are at it again. But when you think about it, it is quite funny… depending on what mother and Crystal end up doing is another story.

The next moment, I hear a short scream from the right hand side near the exit. As I turn to look and see the same young lady called Katie, we have been trying to find out more about. I hear her shout:

"YOU SUCK!!!"

Well that did it by getting mother and Crystal's attention. They suddenly stopped dancing, looking straight over in Katie's direction.

"EXCUSE ME, WHO DO YOU THINK YOU ARE?" shouts Crystal.

Crystal then makes a break for it, running towards Katie, but she vanishes the moment after shouting out. Knowing mother, she will follow suit, so all we can think is, *Here we go again… they're off.*

159

I quickly let Marcus know I am popping outside for a brief moment. Heading through the main dolphin show lobby to the main entrance, I already see Katie running past at god knows what speed, followed by Crystal, and with mother straggling behind at midspeed.

At this point, I quickly think to myself, *Nope, not entertaining this.*

Meanwhile, they all run past in the other direction now, and I turn around, heading back inside to watch the last part of the dolphin show with the boys.

Re-entering through the doors, I take my seat just as they begin the final part of the show, where a few entertainers are dressed as pirates. Damian is really enjoying himself, watching the dolphins jump in and out of the water. The lead entertainer gives a final call, thanking everyone for coming to watch. The crowd cheers and claps as the entertainers exit through the other side. The guests begin to stand up, making their way out of the show area into the main lobby.

"Mum, that was a brilliant show! You missed some of the tricks the dolphins did."

"Sorry son. nan and Crystal decided to start chasing after that young lady. It was bedlam."

"So that's why you went off for a brief moment?"

"Yep, sure was. Are you ready to go home now?"

Growing Up With Secrets

"Yes, I think even Damian is yawning. It has been a great day"

"Let's head back home then son."

"Before we go, I want to stop in the gift shop to get Damian a small cuddly toy."

"Ok son, that's fine. Perhaps a tiger for him?"

"I was thinking of a dolphin, but he can have both."

As we walk towards the gift shop entrance to pick up the tiger and dolphin cuddly toys for Damian. He has already fallen asleep in his pushchair, I pass the toys to the cashier and pay for both. We then head towards the zoo exit, ready to make our way back home after a great family day out.

As we leave, I glance around and spot the Katie still being chased by Crystal and my mother, darting from one area to the next. *They must be getting tired by now, surely?* I think to myself.

I shake my head and carry on walking with the boys as we exit the zoo.

Daniel Cory & Charleine Shepherd

CHAPTER 13

While I'm sitting at the kitchen table, waiting for the kettle to finish boiling so I can make a cup of coffee before getting started on researching the death of the young lady who died at the zoo, I find myself still wondering why she kept giving mother and Crystal the runaround earlier today, even when we were leaving. Somehow, I need to help her cross over into the light and find closure for any unfinished business that may still be keeping her earthbound.

Hearing the kettle click off after boiling, I suddenly realise how quiet the house is. Marcus and Damian are in the living room, but it feels oddly still. Quickly popping my head around the corner of the door to check on them, I see that they are both fast asleep in the armchair. I gently pick up the blanket from the sofa and lay it over them, trying not to disturb their rest.

Today has been a lot of fun, but also a long one for all of us. Especially with everything I had to deal with regarding this ladies situation after witnessing that tragic premonition of her death.

Walking back into the kitchen, I take the milk from the fridge and pour the hot water into my mug. Now I can finally get started on looking through articles and other sources to piece together the missing parts of this situation. Thinking of the old saying my mum

Growing Up With Secrets

used when she was alive, *"No rest for ghost whisperers,"* I reflect on how hard this gift can be to live with. Mum was amazing at handling these situations, and I begin to wonder how Marcus will adjust when his gift fully opens to the spirit world—and what it will be like for Damian when he gets older.

I sit down at the kitchen table, writing notes about what took place in the premonition to help me map out key details that could be found in articles. Opening the web browser on my laptop, I type in the information regarding Katie's death to find any relevant sources. The search results bring up a long list of various websites with similar reports.

Clicking on the third webpage link, I open a BBC News article with the headline:

19 year old lady dies in a tragic accident at Folly Farm Adventure Park and Zoo during a training session

The article details how people were in a state of panic, calling for urgent help as they stood at the marine viewing window, watching the tragic scene unfold. It explains that the orca whale had started acting aggressively for an unknown reason. According to the marine show supervisor, this was highly unusual behaviour that had never occurred before.

Daniel Cory & Charleine Shepherd

Another article I come across states that the Walker family has still not received closure after the death of their daughter, Katie. The inquest remains open as investigators try to determine why the orca whale turned aggressive. The family is being given as much support as possible.

The report continues, stating that the orca whale has since been moved to a large confinement tank at the back of the marine park, where it is undergoing behavioural testing. Experts hope to find answers, and the family is being kept updated on the investigation's progress. The results of these tests are expected to take several weeks to complete.

Scrolling further, I find another article dated 10th August 1993. Clicking on it, I discover a breakthrough in the case. The report explains that the Walker family has finally been given answers about why the orca whale's behaviour was out of character on the day Katie was training. Investigators found that Lummi, the orca, had suffered a slight head injury caused possibly from hitting its head against the tank. Katie had not noticed this when she went to fetch the buckets of fish. The family was relieved to finally understand what had caused the tragedy.

Growing Up With Secrets

In honour of Katie's memory, Folly Farm Adventure Park and Zoo announced they would hold a small memorial service on **15th August 1993 at 13:00 pm**, inviting all guests to attend.

After writing down the key details from the articles, I prepare myself to explain everything to Katie, hoping it will help her understand what really happened that day. However, this may be difficult for her to accept. First, I need to get her here and I'm hoping Crystal and mother can kindly encourage her to come through without any mad dramas kicking off.

"Mother, Crystal, can you come here, please? I need to ask you to do something."

The next moment, they just appear out of nowhere, with strange smiles on their faces as if they've committed a crime.

"Yes darling, you called for us. Is everything ok?"

"All good mum. Why are you both smiling like that? Seriously, what have you done now?"

"Nothing at all, sweetie. What do you need?"

"Hmmm ok. Can you both try to convince Katie to come and see me, please? I've been digging around to find more information about what happened when she died."

Daniel Cory & Charleine Shepherd

"Sure, we'll get her for you Julia. If she isn't rude and, I quote what she said to us, *'You suck.'* She can be rather irritating and stubborn. Even Shaz will tell you the same thing!"

"Ask her nicely, Crystal. She may not be rude to you. Honestly, with you two, anything could happen!"

"Anyway sweet, we'll go and see if Katie will agree to come and see you. Come along Crystal, let's go."

"Thanks Mum. I appreciate you both helping me out."

"You're very welcome. We'll be back soon."

While I wait for mother and Crystal to see if they can convince Katie to come over, I glance up at the clock and see that it's already **18:00 pm**. Time to get some dinner started and then wake the boys from their afternoon slumber. I prep some potatoes and vegetables to go with the mince beef and onion pie from the freezer. I also clear my laptop and notebook off the table to make room for the plates and cutlery, ready for when it's time to dish up the food. It's been half hour when I glance at the clock, thinking it times to wake the boys up, heading out the kitchen into the living room, I then give Marcus a gentle shake to wake him up.

"Son it's time to wake up, dinner will be ready in 10 minutes."

"We will be right there mum."

Growing Up With Secrets

Next minute I am hearing the pitter patter of Damian's feet running towards the kitchen, I turn around, pick him up, and place him in his high chair. Marcus follows a few seconds later, asking, "What's for dinner mum?"

"We're having chicken pie with potatoes and vegetables. Would you like a drink, son?"

"Yes please mum. Could I have a cup of tea?"

"Of course you can. I'll get that now for you and a drink for Damian too. Did you both have a good sleep?"

"It was refreshing to have an afternoon nap mum."

"That's good!"

After giving Marcus and Damian their drinks, I start dishing up dinner. I put Damian's food in his bowl to cool down a little before giving it to him. Placing a plate in front of Marcus and setting mine down at my spot, I put the pots in the sink to soak while we eat. After checking Damian's food, I place it in front of him with his spoon.

As I sit down to start my dinner, I begin explaining to Marcus what I found out today about the young lady from the zoo. He briefly looks at me with a shocked expression but continues eating. After finishing his mouthful, he says, "That poor lady mum. What you saw must have been very distressing. You always know how to help these people who remain stuck earthbound."

"Yes, it's not easy, but once you get the hang of understanding the situation, the hardest part is speaking to the family."

"Mum, are you going to speak with the parents of the young lady to tell them she's stuck and unable to find peace?"

"Yes son, I will do. Unfortunately, there's no other way to help her cross over."

"I admire the work you do mum."

"Thank you son. We'll work on strengthening your gift so you'll be able to help out."

"That would be great mum. I really feel like there's more I could do to help you."

"We'll take it one step at a time son. Your nan would be speaking with you all the time. Some of the things I see can be really funny."

As we finish dinner, Marcus places the plates and bowl on the side, ready to be washed up. He then walks over to Damian, picks him up out of the high chair, and heads upstairs to give him a quick bath before bedtime.

Growing Up With Secrets

I walk over to the sink, take the washing-up liquid from the cupboard, and pour a few drops into the sink. Turning on the tap, I let the water fill the sink, ready to wash the plates, bowl, and cups.

While washing up one of the plates, mother suddenly appears next to me with a concerned look on her face, like something is bothering her. I quickly finish washing up and place everything on the draining rack. Turning around, I see Crystal sitting at the kitchen table, staring at me with the same expression as mother. Neither of them has said anything yet, but then glance at each other.

Something doesn't feel right. The energy around them is unsettling, making me increasingly concerned.

"What's going on with you both? Where is Katie? Can either of you tell me what on earth has happened?"

"Darling, something strange happened when we found Katie. We asked her to come and see you. The next moment, we noticed a dark spirit looming around the zoo not long after we found her," says Mother.

"It saw us all, then suddenly appeared behind us, grabbing hold of Katie. It told us, *'Don't interfere,'* before vanishing with her," Crystal explains.

169

"Oh dear, this does not sound good. Can you both go back and see if there is any trace left from Katie and this dark spirit's energy, please? But be careful."

"We'll be back as quickly as possible hun. It shouldn't take us too long to find a trace of any energy left over."

While waiting anxiously, I begin thinking about where this dark spirit has come from, why it wanted to take Katie, and why it told mother and Crystal not to interfere. But what does it all mean? That's the question.

I walk back to the sink, pull the plug to drain the water, and then dry all the plates, bowl, cutlery, and cups before putting them away.

Sitting down at the table, I open my laptop to search for anything that might help with details about the dark spirit or any ghostly happenings at the zoo in recent years. One website, *Newport News* appears in the search results. It relates to the spooky goings-on and a haunting at the zoo on **21st March 1976**.

Newport News

30th March 1976

SPOOKY GOINGS-ON SCARING STAFF AT POPULAR ZOO ATTRACTION!

Growing Up With Secrets

In a recent interview with the General Manager at Folly Farm Adventure Park and Zoo, staff have reported feeling very uneasy after closing time on several occasions.

One staff member reported to the General Manager that they were in one of the large storage rooms at the rear of the zoo, where animal food and stock are kept. Feeling uneasy and noticing a cold chill in the air, they suddenly heard loud bangs coming from around the corner at the back.

When the staff member went to investigate, they found no one present. Moments later, they fled the area in fear. Similar incidents have occurred after hours, with multiple staff members experiencing the same unsettling events.

The cause of these eerie disturbances remains a mystery with no explanation!

Thinking about my next step, I now need to look further into this situation regarding the dark spirit. Finding out where it has originated from and why it took Katie. This will involve going down to the zoo and speaking with the current General Manager to see if they know anything about past incidents experienced by staff members.

Suddenly, mother and Crystal appear looking very shaken after their visit to the zoo to investigate where the dark spirit was lurking.

Daniel Cory & Charleine Shepherd

From the looks on their faces, I get the feeling this is going to be a challenge already.

"What happened when you went back to find where this dark spirit hides at the zoo?"

"Julia, we went back to where Katie was taken from next to the gift shop. Out of nowhere, it appeared lurking, so we followed it and watched as it headed towards a storage cupboard in the marine centre," Crystal explains.

"Darling, we saw Katie as we peeked through the door. The only thing is... this dark spirit has drained her energy," Mother adds.

"Thank you both, I appreciate you going back to find out where it took her. I'm going back tomorrow to speak with the General Manager. For now, you both should rest, as I may need you."

"Can we stay here with you for the night?"

"Of course you both can. I'm going to head upstairs to speak with Marcus and say goodnight to Damian. I'll see you both in the morning."

"Ok love, see you in the morning. Love you lots."

"Love you lots too mum."

"NIGHT JULIA!"

Growing Up With Secrets

"Goodnight Crystal. Don't shout, you'll wake Damian, you bonkers woman!"

After turning off all the lights downstairs, I make my way upstairs, still thinking about this situation and how I now have to deal with a spirit rescue. Reaching the top of the stairs, I walk into Damian's bedroom and see Marcus sitting on a chair, reading a bedtime story to Damian called *Goodnight Stars and Moon.*

I kiss Damian on the forehead. "Goodnight, my precious angel. Have a magical sleep and sweet dreams." Then, I whisper to Marcus, "When you've put Damian down to sleep, come into my room. I need to speak with you about something." Marcus nods in acknowledgment.

Leaving Damian's bedroom, I go straight to the bathroom to brush my teeth before having a chat with Marcus about what's happening with this dark spirit. After finishing, I come out and see Marcus gently closing Damian's door, leaving it slightly open.

"Are we going to sit in your room mum, to have a chat?" he asks.

"Yes son."

Walking into my bedroom, we sit on the bed. I take a deep breath, thinking about where to begin. I need to explain everything from the start. How the dark spirit suddenly appeared kidnapping Katie, and the events that unfolded this evening after dinner.

Daniel Cory & Charleine Shepherd

"Son, nan and Crystal returned to the zoo to ask Katie to come and see me so I could explain what happened to her after the accident. Unfortunately, they saw a dark spirit lurking nearby. It noticed them all talking."

"Oh my goodness! What happened?"

"Nan and Crystal returned with very concerned looks on their faces. They explained that the dark spirit had kidnapped Katie and told them, 'Do not interfere.' I asked them to go back to find any trace of energy left behind by the dark spirit."

"Mum, what does this dark spirit want with Katie? Have you figured out how to rescue her?"

"I've been doing some research and found an article from 1976 about similar incidents reported by staff at the time. We now know where the dark spirit dwells in the zoo, but there's still more to uncover."

"Please be careful mum. It sounds powerful and dangerous!"

"I know son. Until we understand what it wants, I'll have to go back to the zoo tomorrow and speak with the General Manager. For now, let's get some sleep."

"Ok mum. I'll see you in the morning."

"Goodnight son."

Growing Up With Secrets

Marcus walks out of my room, closing the door behind him. I get into bed, turn off the lamp, and finally allow myself to rest.

*****

It's the middle of the night. when, all of a sudden, I am woken by a massive bang coming from downstairs in the living room, where mother and Crystal are resting. I turn on the lamp and quickly get out of bed. As I walk towards the door, Crystal suddenly appears in front of me.

"The dark spirit appeared out of nowhere, threatening us for not listening! I've left Shaz on her own with it. Julia, you have to hurry!"

Crystal vanishes back downstairs. I throw open the bedroom door, switch on the landing light, and race down the stairs into the living room, only to see the dark spirit holding my mother.

"Julia don't come any closer! We don't know what this spirit is capable of," Crystal warns.

I glare at the entity. "Who are you, and what the hell are you doing kidnapping spirits? Let my mother go now or else!"

The spirit laughs menacingly. "What are you going to do, silly woman? They were warned not to come back! Now your mother is mine, just like the girl. This is your last warning: stay away, or else!"

Before I can react, the evil spirit vanishes, taking mother with it.

Daniel Cory & Charleine Shepherd

"NOOOO! MUM! BRING HER BACK!" I scream.

What does it want with both of them? And what did it mean about being warned to stay away? It's all so confusing. I glance at Crystal, seeing she's in a panic, and now, until we rescue mother and Katie, she's completely on her own.

"Julia what are we going to do? This spirit is very strong!"

"Crystal you need to stay calm. We will stop it, I promise. But I need to figure out what's going on at the zoo tomorrow so we can counteract it. We can't do anything about it if we're both exhausted."

"Ok Julia... I guess we should get some rest. The sun will be up soon."

"Indeed my lovely. See you in a few hours."

Heading back upstairs, I notice that neither of the boys has been disturbed by the bang from downstairs. Peeking into their rooms, I see them both still sound asleep. This dark spirit puzzles me more now than ever. Still deep in thought, I walk back into my bedroom, get into bed, and switch off the lamp.

Morning comes too soon. The alarm clock goes off, and I groggily look over to see it's 7:30 am. It's been a stressful night after what happened to mother. How am I going to explain this to Marcus over breakfast?

Growing Up With Secrets

Today, I'll have to go back to the zoo and speak with the General Manager to get more information. Why has this all suddenly started happening again? Something doesn't add up. Whatever took place in the past is repeating now, and it's targeting spirits. I need answers.

Time to get out of bed. I head to the bathroom, then wake the boys before going downstairs to check on Crystal. I also need to get breakfast started as I'll definitely need a strong coffee to get through today.

After coming out of the bathroom, I slowly open Damian's bedroom door and quietly walk in. I go over to his cot and see that he's just beginning to wake, his eyes opening gradually. I lean over, pick him up, and carry him downstairs with me.

As we enter the living room, I see Crystal pacing back and forth, muttering to herself. I'm about to get her attention, but Damian beats me to it when he giggles, making her stop and looks at us both.

"Morning Julia. And good morning to you, little man," she says, managing a small smile.

"Morning Crystal. How are you feeling? I noticed you were pacing and talking to yourself."

Damian giggles again, smiling at Crystal. She pauses for a moment before smiling back at him, then looks at me.

177

"Sorry Julia. I'm doing alright, still worried about Shaz though. That's why I was pacing and talking to myself."

"I was a little worried about you hun, that's all. But we will get mother back! Come to the kitchen with us. Marcus will be down any minute for his coffee too."

"Sure, I'll come with you Julia."

We walk out of the living room just as we see Marcus coming down the stairs in his dressing gown, looking half asleep and completely oblivious to anything around him. We continue into the kitchen, where I place Damian in his high chair. I fill the kettle with fresh water and set it to boil while Marcus pulls out a chair and slumps down, still half asleep.

"Morning son. Would you like a coffee or tea?"

"Mornnning mum. I'm still waking up, please can you make me a strong coffee?"

"Yes, of course son. I've just put the kettle on to boil."

I take the cups out of the cupboard and place them on the countertop next to the kettle. While waiting, I put some coffee in each cup and start preparing breakfast for Damian, along with his morning bottle of milk.

Growing Up With Secrets

I take Damian's bowl out of the cupboard, grab the Ready Brek, and pour a small amount into the bowl. Then, I get the milk from the fridge, add a little to the Ready Brek powder, and place the bowl in the microwave for one minute, just enough to warm it. I'll take a small taste when it's ready to make sure it isn't too hot.

The kettle clicks. I pour the hot water into both mine and Marcus's cups, then take them to the table along with Damian's bottle just as the microwave dings. I open the microwave, take out the bowl, and check the temperature with a small spoonful. It's perfect. As I place the bowl in front of Damian, he gives me a cheeky giggle.

Handing Marcus his cup, I sit down at the table with a small plate of biscuits. I need to explain to him everything that happened in the early hours of this morning regarding the dark spirit kidnapping nan.

"Son, I need to tell you about this incident in the house during the early hours. Nan was kidnapped by the dark spirit."

"What happened? What dark spirit mum?"

"You remember the young lady called Katie, whom I was trying to help? She was taken by the dark spirit too. At the zoo, right in front of nan and Crystal. But after they went back to try and find her. The dark spirit appeared in front of them both and warned them that if they got involved, there would be serious consequences. But, as you know nan and Crystal won't listen when it comes to finding out information.

They went back to the zoo storage room out the back, searching for any trace of Katie, and the dark spirit followed them back not long after."

"OMG! Mum, what are you going to do?"

"Well son, I was thinking of going back to the zoo to speak with the General Manager. I need to investigate previous incidents involving this dark spirit. But there's something else that happened in the early hours of this morning."

"What happened mum?"

"At 3:00 am, I heard a massive bang coming from the living room, where nan and Crystal were resting. I got out of bed and walked towards the door. As I opened it, Crystal appeared in a terrible state, telling me to hurry downstairs to nan. I rushed down to find the dark spirit in the living room, it had hold of your Nan. Before I could do anything, it vanished... taking her with it."

I see the worry and fear in his eyes. I need to reassure him that I will do everything in my power to get this sorted and rescue both mother and Katie. This dark spirit's reign of terror and disruption at the zoo, along with its kidnapping of peaceful spirits, has to end.

"Don't worry son. I'll get this all sorted and rescue nan!"

"Mum, is there anything I can do to help?"

Growing Up With Secrets

"For now, just look after Damian. This isn't something you're ready to deal with."

"Ok mum... Please be careful when you go to stop this spirit. I just worry something bad will happen."

"I'll be alright son. This isn't the first spirit I've dealt with."

"Please keep me updated."

"Of course son. No problem at all. I know it'll give you peace of mind."

"Thank you mum. Love you loads."

"Love you loads too son."

I get up from the table, put my cup in the sink, and head upstairs to have a wash and get dressed.

When I come back downstairs into the living room, I notice Crystal sitting there, lost in deep thought. I wonder what's going through her mind.

"Are you alright, Crystal? You seem very distant. Anything I can help with?"

"Oh, hi Julia. I was just thinking about everything that's happened... and what I could do to help."

"Don't worry lovely. We will get this situation resolved. Hang in there, I will need your help. But first, I need to make a plan. So chin up, ok?"

"Ok... I'll do my best Julia."

"You'll be fine, I promise."

My plan of action will be to use my hidden ability to drain the dark spirit of its energy, creating a light seal while using angelic white light chains to trap it, then send it back to the dark dimension of the spirit world. Crystal will need to act as a decoy to gain the spirit's attention first, allowing me to act quickly. I'll check with her first to make sure she's ok with that.

"Crystal, can I ask if you would be the decoy, by distracting the dark spirit's attention?"

"Yes, of course Julia. Anything I can do to help."

"Brilliant. This will allow me to activate a light seal, encasing the dark spirit in light chains to drain its energy before I send it back to the dark dimension."

"That's brilliant! I never knew you had this hidden ability."

"It's very rare that I need to use it, which is why I've never told anyone about it."

Growing Up With Secrets

"I've never seen anything like this before. It'll be amazing to see it in action."

It's time to head to the zoo for my appointment with the General Manager. Hopefully, he might have some information about the dark spirit. I pick up my bag and head into the kitchen to grab my notebook and the case file on Katie that I've put together.

Marcus is already upstairs with Damian, getting him sorted for the day, so I call up the stairs to let him know I'm heading out.

"Marcus, I'm off to my appointment at the zoo. I'll see you both later. If you need anything, call my mobile."

"Ok mum. We'll see you later. Hope you get the situation sorted."

"Byeeee! See you both later."

I open the front door, step outside, and close it behind me before heading towards to the car. Unlocking the door, I get inside, start the engine, and reverse out of the driveway.

Time to begin my journey to the zoo.

***

Arriving in the zoo car park, I pull into one of the spaces close to the building. I open the car door, step out, lock the car, and head towards the reception building. As I approach the main entrance and push the door open, I sense a strange energy lingering. Ignoring it for

Daniel Cory & Charleine Shepherd

now, I continue towards the reception desk to ask about seeing the General Manager.

The receptionist looks a little nervous as she calls the General Manager on the phone. As I glance towards the doorway leading from reception into the main part of the zoo, I suddenly see the dark spirit walking past. In an instant, it vanishes. I feel relieved that it didn't notice me standing here. It does explains the strange energy I picked up on when entering the building.

The receptionist hangs up the phone and turns to me.

"I have spoken to the General Manager. He will be out in five minutes. Is there anything else I can help you with?"

"I just wanted to ask, have you seen or heard anything unusual happening here?"

"Yes, I experienced something very strange during my lunch break the other day, near the rear of the park opposite the staff canteen. There was loud banging coming from a storage cupboard, so I went to check what was happening."

"What happened?"

"I felt like I was being watched... then something called my name, yet no one was there! I ran out, absolutely terrified, and I haven't been near there since."

Growing Up With Secrets

"Oh no, I'm so sorry that happened to you. If I can provide any support, please let me know."

"Thank you, that's very kind."

"You're welcome. I'll get to the bottom of what's happening here. I'm sure the General Manager can shed more light on the matter."

About ten minutes pass before I see the General Manager walking towards the reception desk, a concerned look on his face. I wonder what's going through his mind.

"Hello madam. My name is Douglas Fitzgerald. How may I help you today?"

"Hello, I'm Julia Jones. I was hoping you could help me with an enquiry. I'm currently investigating the strange occurrences happening here at the zoo. Are you able to shed any light on the matter?"

"Of course. Please follow me to my office. You can call me Doug, and I'll make us a cup of coffee while we chat."

"Sounds great, Doug. Thank you for your time, I really appreciate it."

As we walk through the main part of the zoo, we turn left and enter another building with a sign on the door reading *Private – Staff Only*. Inside, the hallway leads past several offices and a small meeting room's. The first door is labelled *General Manager's Office*. Doug

185

Daniel Cory & Charleine Shepherd

opens the door, and as we step inside, he heads straight towards a neatly arranged tea and coffee station.

"Julia, how do you take your coffee?"

"Black, with two sugars please."

"Let's have a chat while we wait for the kettle to boil, it takes forever!"

"No problem at all, take your time."

Watching Doug from where I'm sitting, I notice his energy shift slightly. There's a hint of worry as he prepares the coffee. The kettle rattles as it comes to a boil, and when it clicks off, he pours the hot water into both cups and brings them over.

"Hope this is ok for you Julia."

"It's perfect, thank you."

"I need to ask you to keep an open mind about what I'm about to tell you."

"Of course, that's fine."

"I have a special gift, I can see and communicate with the dead. There's a dark spirit that has been lurking around this zoo for a while. It kidnapped my mother and a young girl named Katie and is holding them hostage. I can show you a newspaper article from 30th March 1976."

Growing Up With Secrets

"Of course Julia. I remember staff reporting incidents about this years ago."

Handing Doug the newspaper article, I watch as he silently reads through it. His facial expression shifts to deep concern, confirming that he understands the gravity of the situation. It explains the strong sense of worry I had picked up in his energy.

After a few moments, he looks up.

"Julia, to shed some light on this, we've had several staff members report disturbing experiences after hours around the zoo grounds. They've seen a dark shadow lurking, only for it to vanish into thin air. Some have had terrifying encounters in the large storage room at the back of the zoo. One staff member heard loud banging, then their name being called, but no one was there. Another reported a sudden drop in temperature, followed by a chilling voice shouting: 'GET OUT NOW!' Both of them refused to go near the area again and eventually left the company. It's been going on for years now but no one goes there alone anymore, only in pairs or small groups."

"I'm able to help find a solution to get rid of this dark spirit. I need to finish some research at home. Can we schedule a time out of hours when the zoo is closed so I can perform a spiritual clearing?"

"Of course, Julia. We can arrange an evening next week. How does Wednesday at 19:30 sound?"

Daniel Cory & Charleine Shepherd

"Perfect. I'll get everything sorted at home and prepare for later. Can you take me down to the storage cupboard where these incidents have been reported?"

"Yes, for sure. Let's head over there now."

"Thank you Doug."

"Happy to help Julia."

Doug places both cups on the tray beside the kettle as I stand up and make my way towards the door. He opens it, and I follow him down the corridor as we make our way towards the location where these terrifying incidents have taken place.

As we arrive at the storage room, I immediately sense a strong energy essence coming from the dark spirit. I quickly scan the area, ensuring it isn't lurking nearby. When I push the handle down, the door opens. This has remained unlocked since the last person fled in fear, and no other staff members have dared to return.

Walking into the archive room, I see stacks of boxes scattered around, along with other items spread between three aisles of compact shelving units. The air feels heavy, carrying a sense of unsettled energy. Then, out of the corner of my eye, I notice a box protruding from the bottom shelf, labelled *Archived Staff Incidents and Records*.

"Doug, would it be okay if I looked inside? There might be information about past encounters with the dark spirit."

Growing Up With Secrets

"Of course, that's fine."

As I reach into the box and touch one of the files, it triggers a sudden premonition. I am taken back to a time in the past, where I see an older female staff member frozen in fear. Before her, the dark spirit has taken on a terrifying form of something I've never seen before, even when encountering it at home. It looks like a monstrous beast with horns and glowing red eyes. As the vision fades, I catch a glimpse of the woman's name badge: *Siobhan Baxter – Park Assistant.*

Doug's voice brings me back to reality.

"Julia, are you alright?"

"Yes, I'm fine. This happens when I have premonitions."

"What did you see?"

"When I touched one of the files, I saw a vision of the past. The dark spirit had taken on a beast like form and was cornering a young woman named Siobhan, a park assistant. She was paralysed with fear. Do you have a file on her?"

"Oh, that's not good… She must have worked here a long time ago. I can't remember the exact year, but her file should be in the box."

"Thanks Doug. Would it be alright if I took the box home to go through the records in more detail?"

"No problem, Julia. If it makes things easier for you, of course you can."

"It will be much easier to read through everything at home. Doug, please take down my home number in case you need to contact me."

"Thank you. Let me walk you back to the main building."

As we make our way through the zoo grounds, we discuss my plan to banish the dark spirit once and for all. When we reach the main building, I shift the archive box into my arms and turn to Doug.

"Thank you for your help today. I'll give you a call tomorrow once I've gone through the records."

"That's fine, Julia. Your help is very much appreciated."

"Anytime, it's a pleasure to assist. Take care for now."

"Bye Julia."

Exiting the zoo's main building, I cross the car park. When I reach my car, I set the box down on the ground while unlocking the boot. I then lift the box inside, close the boot door, and get into the car, ready to drive home.

***

Pulling up outside the house, I turn off the car and open the door to step out. Walking to the rear of the car, I open the boot and lift out the archive box. After locking the car, I head down the pathway,

Growing Up With Secrets

noticing how quiet the house seems, like there is no sign of life. I wonder if the boys have gone out.

Placing the box down for a moment, I unlock the front door, then lift the box again and step inside, closing the door behind me. Just then, I hear the TV on in the living room. As I pass by, I glance in to see Marcus and Damian cuddled up asleep together in the armchair. Smiling at the sight, I continue into the kitchen, setting the records box down on the table.

I fill the kettle with water, preparing to make myself a cup of coffee before waking the boys. Turning around, I suddenly realise the slow cooker is on, and the rich aroma of beef stew fills the air, and it smells amazing. A moment later, the kettle clicks off, and I pour the hot water into my cup before sitting down at the table. I open the box and pull out the file on Siobhan Baxter, eager to see if there is any information that confirms what I saw in my vision at the storage room.

Reading through the incident report, I learn that Siobhan had gone to the storage cupboard to fetch extra birdseed for the enclosure when she was startled by unknown noises and a low voice calling her name, yet no one was there. Moments later, something dashed past the corner of her eye, like a dark shadow.

On her way back with the bag of birdseed, she reported hearing banging sounds coming from inside the storage archive room.

Daniel Cory & Charleine Shepherd

Concerned, she unlocked and opened the door to investigate. After walking past two aisles of shelving cabinets, a cold sensation came over her, and suddenly she saw a box shift out from the far end of the shelving unit.

Siobhan found the box on the bottom shelf, seemingly having moved by itself. She placed it back, but when she turned around, the dark spirit appeared. It began transforming into a monstrous beast, cornering her in the room and leaving her frozen in fear. The report does not explain what the entity wanted, but it seems intent on making its presence known, scaring off anyone who comes near this area of the zoo. The last note in the report states that after the spirit vanished without a trace, Siobhan fled in terror, leaving the door unlocked. She was so shaken that she resigned with immediate effect, unwilling to continue working at the zoo.

I pull out other files containing similar reports from staff who have seen the dark spirit appear and disappear within seconds. These articles help me understand that I am dealing with a demon entity that prefers to take human form. Once I seal this dark spirit away in the dark dimension of the spirit world, we can safely rescue mother and Katie, restoring peace to the zoo after all the chaos.

Plan of Action to Stop the Dark Spirit:

- Use white chalk to draw a binding circle.

Growing Up With Secrets

- Trap the dark spirit once it crosses into the circle, encasing it in light chains.
- Crystal acts as bait to lure the spirit into the trap.
- Recite the banishment incantation.
- Rescue Mother and Katie.
- Perform a quick, wide scale spiritual cleansing.

I decide to call the zoo to see if Doug is available, so I can explain my plan in detail and arrange a suitable evening, preferably out of hours, to ensure no staff are around.

"Hello, Folly Adventure Zoo and Park. How can I help?"

"Hi, could I speak with Doug, the general manager, please?"

"I'll have to check if he's available. May I ask who's calling?"

"Thank you. It's Julia Jones."

"One moment, please hold Julia."

A few moments later, Doug picks up the call.

"Hello Julia! How are you?"

"Hi Doug. I'm doing well. I just wanted to let you know that I've come up with a plan to get rid of the dark spirit. Would it be possible to schedule an evening to attend after hours, when the park is closed, so I can perform the cleansing?"

Daniel Cory & Charleine Shepherd

"Yes, we can indeed. Shall we say tomorrow at 19:00 at the main gate?"

"Perfect. I'll bring everything along tomorrow evening and return the archive box as well."

"Super! I look forward to seeing you tomorrow, Julia."

"Thanks Doug. See you tomorrow. Bye."

"Bye Julia."

After putting the phone down, I walk into the living room to wake up the boys, as I need to explain the plans for returning to the zoo tomorrow evening to finally resolve this problem with the dark spirit. Giving Marcus a gentle nudge, I see that even Damian is beginning to stir.

"Marcus, it's time to wake up son."

"Ohh mum, it's you. When did you get back home?"

"About an hour ago son. I need to let you know about the plans for tomorrow."

"What's happening tomorrow mum?"

"I'll be returning to the zoo tomorrow evening around 19:00 to finally resolve the problem with this dark spirit. I also need to explain the entire situation to Crystal, as she'll be acting as the decoy to lure the dark spirit into the holding circle."

Growing Up With Secrets

"Mum, please take care when you go tomorrow!"

"I will son."

"Julia, let's do this and get that dark spirit packing! WOOOOO!"

"Blimey Crystal! You're bursting with energy. Did you overhear the conversation?"

"Yeah, I was standing in the hallway. I like the plan, Julia."

"We'll chat about it in more detail later this evening Crystal."

"No worries at all Julia. When you need me, just shout!"

"Will do Crystal. Son, do you want me to take Damian so you can get dinner sorted?"

"Yes please mum. You can both spend some time together. I'll give you a shout when I'm about to dish up."

Marcus heads off to the kitchen to prepare dinner while I get to spend some quality time with my special grandson. I haven't felt like I've been around much for him lately, having to deal with this dark spirit situation. Damian hands me his stuffed tiger toy, so I make some light growling noises.

"Grrrrr, rawrrr, grrrrr!"

He giggles. "Nanny, you sound like a tiger!"

That moment cheers up my evening. It feels good to see Damian enjoying our time together before dinner.

Daniel Cory & Charleine Shepherd

"Mum, I'm going to start dishing up now."

Getting up off the sofa, I pick Damian up, and we make our way into the kitchen. Another whiff of the amazing beef stew Marcus has made fills the air. I put Damian into his highchair and bring our drinks over from the kitchen counter as Marcus carries the dinner bowls to the table.

"Wow, dinner looks so tasty son! Can't wait to dig in."

"Enjoy mum. It has a special blend of gentle seasoning to bring out a great taste."

We all sit quietly, eating dinner. My mind drifts to thoughts of mother and Katie, wondering what might be happening to them while they are being held captive by the dark spirit. It must have them hidden somewhere in the zoo, masking their energy traces. It won't be long before we head back to the zoo, but I'll need a good night's sleep to be at full strength for banishing the entity back into the spirit world.

"Son, I just wanted to compliment you on that lovely stew you made. It was amazing."

"Glad you liked it mum. Looks like Damian enjoyed it too!"

"There's nothing left in his bowl, bless his little heart. He's a growing boy indeed."

"Very true indeed."

Growing Up With Secrets

Marcus takes all our bowls, placing them on the side while filling the sink with warm water and adding a little washing-up liquid. I get Damian out of his highchair and take him over to Marcus so he can give him a goodnight kiss before I take him upstairs to get ready for bed.

We walk out of the kitchen and head upstairs to Damian's room. Once inside, I sit him down while he clutches his tiger toy. As I put his pyjamas on, Crystal pops in to say goodnight to him as well. After laying him down in the cot, I turn on the star shaped night light. Leaning down, I kiss Damian on his forehead and wish him a good night's sleep with sweet dreams. As I walk out of the room, I pull the door slightly to before heading downstairs.

Walking into the living room, I see Crystal already sitting on the sofa waiting for me. Blimey, I think, it must be fun to vanish and appear suddenly in different places. I sit down next to her and begin explaining the details of our plan for tomorrow evening at the zoo.

"We'll head straight to the location and draw the binding circle with white chalk first. After that, we'll set off to locate the dark spirit. But we need to be extra vigilant to ensure everything is on point. This isn't any normal spirit we're dealing with. I saw in a past vision that it takes the form of a demon beast entity."

"No problem Julia. I'll make sure to follow the plan exactly as required."

"Thank you again for all your help, Crystal. Couldn't do it without you!"

"Always here anytime, you know that Julia. Popping out for a bit, see you shortly."

"Ok Crystal. See you later."

Just as she vanishes, Marcus walks into the living room holding two cups of decaf tea. He hands one to me before sitting down in the armchair. I take a sip and mention the situation to him, explaining that Crystal and I will be heading to the zoo tomorrow night on a rescue mission.

"I've explained everything in detail to Crystal about tomorrow. By the end of it, the dark spirit should be gone, and we'll be coming back with nan and Katie."

"Mum, I'm really worried about you both going. It sounds like a very dangerous situation!"

"Trust me son, it will work out in the best way possible. I've checked through the plans to make sure we stay vigilant and follow everything through correctly."

"That helps calm my nerves a little. Love you loads mum."

Growing Up With Secrets

"Love you loads too son."

After we finish our tea, I take both mugs to the kitchen and leave them in the sink, ready for washing up in the morning. We then head upstairs to bed, ready to get some rest before tomorrow.

CHAPTER 14

I wake up and glance over at the clock to see it's only 6:30 am. The thought hits me, realising today has finally arrived. The day to banish the dark spirit, then rescue mum and Katie. As I think about it, I can't help but hope they're both alright, wherever they might be held.

Pulling back the covers, I get out of bed and straighten the duvet, making it look tidy. I pick up my dressing gown from the end of the bed, put it on, and head downstairs. As I step out of the bedroom onto the landing, an overwhelming heavy feeling suddenly comes over me, triggering another vision.

In the vision, I see the dark spirit taking its beast form, chasing Crystal through the zoo. Somehow, it knows we are planning to stop it from causing any more trouble.

When the vision ends, I notice how the heavy energy vanishes without a trace. Oh my, what a dreadful feeling that was. Something tells me this wasn't just a normal vision and it was a warning, showing me in advance what's about to take place. The only good thing about this, it allows me to anticipate the dark spirit's movements and adjust the plan to prevent it from being foiled. It's great to be a Psychic Medium with these amazing gifts.

Growing Up With Secrets

As I stand on the landing, Crystal suddenly appears, having sensed the surge of negative energy rippling through the spirit world.

"Julia, are you alright? I felt a horrible presence rushing through the spirit world."

"Yes, I'm alright. I had a warning vision about the dark spirit."

"Oh my, that doesn't sound good. Does the dark spirit know we're coming?"

"It has an idea that we're planning something, but it's ok we can slightly adjust the plan."

"Julia, we are going to win."

"We will indeed Crystal. I'm heading downstairs, I need a coffee."

Crystal vanishes before my very eyes, like a sudden gust of wind. She really doesn't give it much thought when she does that, even in the middle of a conversation. I chuckle to myself, thinking she needs a new nickname, The Swift Vanisher seems like a perfect fit for this loony woman.

Still smiling, I make my way downstairs, walk through the hallway, and enter the kitchen. Clicking the kettle on, I get my cup ready for a strong coffee. Once the kettle finishes boiling, I pour the hot water into the cup and place the kettle back on its stand. Picking up my coffee, I head to the living room, sit down in the armchair, and read over the plan.

I make one slight adjustment where Crystal will use her vanishing and reappearing trick to avoid the dark spirit catching her, making it easier to lure it towards the banishment circle with no escape. Having that vision was actually useful, it's allowed me to make this crucial change. The dark spirit thinks it's going to trip us up, but it won't.

Crystal reappears on the sofa while I'm sitting in the armchair. I immediately notice that she looks rather concerned.

"What's bothering you, Crystal?" I ask.

"Julia, please don't be mad at me. I went back to the zoo this morning while you were fast asleep to have a nose around."

"Oh my, are you ok? The dark spirit didn't see you, did it?"

"Not at all. I learned how to hide my energy trace before entering, so I didn't raise its attention. I hid behind one of the buildings, watching it pass by. I followed it back to where Shaz and Katie are being held captive."

"Wow Crystal, you're amazingly brilliant! Where abouts are they?"

Growing Up With Secrets

"They're currently inside an energy bound cage located behind the tiger enclosure, in a large room mostly used for storing cleaning items."

"Great! When we go tonight, I'll set up the ritual circle in another part of the zoo. And remember to use your vanishing tricks, they'll definitely help!"

"I'll remember Julia. You can count on me!"

"Thank you, Crystal. We are good to go for tonight."

"You're welcome, Julia. Give me a shout when you need me later."

Before I can say anything else, Crystal vanishes again, leaving me completely baffled. How does she do that?

Now that time is moving on, I'd best check what we're having for breakfast. I know the boys will be waking up soon, even though it's only 7:00 am.

Another thought hits me realising Marcus is due back at work in a couple of days. It's vital that we sort this situation out tonight, bringing mum and Katie back safely.

I open the kitchen cupboard and spot a box of Weetabix. That'll do perfectly. We don't often have something different, but it'll make a nice change. I pick up some bananas from the fruit bowl to slice and place on top. Leaving everything on the kitchen counter, I decide it's time to go upstairs, get washed, and get dressed. It should be around 7:30 am now.

First, I pop into Damian's room to wake him up. Peering into the cot, I see the cheeky little monster is already awake, giggling and smiling as he must have heard me coming up. Picking him up, I carry him with me to wake Marcus, even though I can already hear his snoring through the slightly open door.

Pushing it open, I walk in and call, "Son, it's time to wake up now."

"Ohh, morning mum. What time is it?"

"7:35 am. Damian was awake as I walked into him."

"Two seconds mum. Let me get up, put my dressing gown on, and I'll take Damian."

"Thanks son. I've got breakfast ready to start with everything is on the kitchen counter."

"Come on little man. Nanny's going to get breakfast ready for us. Yay, we will follow!"

"See you downstairs in a second son."

Walking out of Marcus's room, I make my way down the stairs and into the kitchen to get breakfast started. I sort everything out by placing one Weetabix in Damian's bowl and two in each of the other

Growing Up With Secrets

bowls, leaving mine until last. Fetching the milk, I pour a little on each and break it down before placing them all in the microwave for one minute and thirty seconds. While those heat up, I start cutting the banana into small slices, ready to place on top.

Marcus walks into the kitchen with Damian, sitting him in the highchair before taking a seat at the table himself. Just as the microwave dings, I check to make sure the Weetabix isn't too hot. It seems warm but not too hot, so I remove the bowls and bring them over, adding the banana slices on top. Handing the bowls to Marcus and Damian, they both tuck in.

The kettle finishes boiling, so I quickly pour hot water into my cup, mix in some milk, and prepare a small beaker of milk for Damian. I pop both on the table for them while sorting out my own breakfast. Finally, I sit down to join the boys at the table.

While we're sitting here, a thought crosses my mind, I might as well ask Marcus when he's due back at work so I can note it on the calendar.

"Son, can I ask which day you'll be back at work this week?"

"I'm due back on Thursday, just getting back into a routine again after being off for a while."

Daniel Cory & Charleine Shepherd

"Indeed son. Damian will be starting nursery soon too, that's coming around fast."

"What date does he start nursery mum? Sorry, I probably haven't kept up with everything recently."

"If I remember correctly, Damian starts on Monday, 5th September 1994. I'll double-check the calendar shortly."

"That'll be good for him. Providing some time for socialising and learning."

"Indeed, it will son. To be honest, Damian picks things up fast. That's something I've really noticed."

"Now you mention it, so true. That's our boy! Thanks for breakfast too mum, it was delicious!"

"You're very welcome. Looks like my little man is finished too. Do you both want to go get washed and dressed while I clear everything up?"

"Yes of course, no problem. Come on my little man, let's go get ourselves sorted."

Marcus walks out of the kitchen with Damian to get washed and dressed for the day ahead while I clean up and put everything back in its place.

Growing Up With Secrets

I wonder if Crystal is doing alright this morning after leaving so suddenly. I just hope she hasn't gotten into any trouble or gone near the zoo, stirring up the dark spirit. If she gets caught, all hell will break loose, making it even trickier to stop it.

After finishing the washing-up, I head back into the living room to sit down for a couple of minutes and read the morning paper.

Just as I open it to the first page, Crystal appears beside me, scaring the life out of me! Where on earth has she been? Judging by the sound of her voice, she seems really happy. Like she's just caused some sort of havoc. Which, knowing her, it's probably true.

"Hey Julia! Whatcha doing?"

"Jeez woman! Don't do that, how many times?!"

"Sorry about that! Were you busy? I need to tell you something that I found out. Some new information that I think will help us tonight."

"Apart from trying to read the paper, but that doesn't matter now. What have you found out? And where have you been?"

"Well, I went back to the zoo, where Shaz and Katie are being kept. I saw the dark spirit leave the room in human form as it walked through a wall into another building. So, I sneaked in to speak with them both and make sure they're alright."

"That's good! What did you find out?"

"Shaz was open but worried about the dark spirit is getting stronger from feeding on negative energy and scaring people. Katie seems a bit secluded in her own world, not talking much. The cage they're in is somehow linked to the dark spirit's energy, so once we banish it, the cage will vanish too."

"Brilliant Crystal! You found something extra we can use against it!"

"You're welcome, Julia! Oh, look here comes Marcus with Damian in his arms."

Marcus walks into the living room with Damian. I immediately notice Crystal waving at him, and I hear giggling. That's the moment it happens. Marcus starts to hear Crystal's voice for the first time, his gift of hearing finally opening up.

Although it shocks him a little, we weren't expecting this to happen just yet. But we knew his ability would grow with practice. But it seems to be unfolding naturally.

"Mum, who is that I'm hearing? And what's going on right now?"

"Don't panic son. Your gift of hearing ghosts has opened naturally. You're hearing Crystal right now and she's saying hello to Damian."

"OHHH, NO WAY! HE CAN HEAR ME?!"

Growing Up With Secrets

"Hello Crystal! It's nice to meet you. Sorry I can't see you just yet. My gift hasn't fully developed. I've heard a lot about the great things you've done helping my mum, and I just want to say a massive thank you."

"It's a pleasure indeed, helping tonight with getting rid of this dark spirit to rescue your nan and the other lady called Katie."

"Please take care tonight when you're both going."

"We will for sure Marcus, I promise!!"

"Mum, I'll take Damian out in his pushchair to the park for an hour at about 11:00 am."

"Sure son, no problem. Did you want to sort out some lunch when you return, or we could pop out to the local café?"

"Yeah, let's pop to the café when we're back, that will be nice for a change."

"It's a plan son."

While Crystal is sitting on the floor playing with Damian, I pick up the morning newspaper to finish reading an article about a ghostly haunting. It describes how a group of people went exploring an old abandoned mental hospital in West Yorkshire. It didn't take long before they were all running out after hearing unknown screams and bangs echoing through the dark corridors.

Daniel Cory & Charleine Shepherd

The next moment, a wheelchair apparently started rolling forward, then suddenly picked up full speed. Almost as if it was powered by some extreme battery that was charging straight towards them. With sheer luck, they managed to shove themselves against the wall just in time, watching as it speed past and straight round a corner into another room before crashing.

Looks like another place for me to investigate.

Perhaps when Marcus's gift is stronger, he might want to come along with me for this one. Although I'm not sure how he'd feel about leaving Damian at Laura's for a few days. I suppose I'll cross that bridge when we come to it. We haven't really been in touch for a while. We have not heard anything since the last incident when mother and Crystal decided to haunt their place, causing havoc, then conveniently failed to mention it to me.

Turning to the horoscope page, I check what's in the stars today. I find the section and read through Cancer, Leo, and Taurus, all sounding rather positive, though of course they're always general for a lot of people.

After finishing, I close the newspaper, fold it neatly, and place it back in the magazine rack.

Growing Up With Secrets

Getting up from the armchair, I briefly get the calendar asit needs some new entries, especially noting Marcus's return to work and Damian's nursery start date.

***

While Marcus gets the pushchair set up, I put Damian's coat on him, ready to go to the park for an hour.

"Are you going out for a morning adventure with your dad, my little man?" I say, watching him giggle at me with excitement.

"Mum the pushchair is up and ready."

"Ok son. Here we go, my little man. Ready, steady, goooo!"

That gets us all laughing as I sit Damian in the pushchair, clip the straps in place, and make sure they're both good to go. Opening the front door, I watch as Marcus heads out, pushing the buggy. I can feel a light breeze in the air, carrying the fresh scent of grass from the nearby fields where some horses graze. They belong to the local riding school just up the road. Ah, the beauty of Wales at its finest.

"See you shortly mum. We'll be back soon."

"Have a good time son. See you both in a little while."

As Marcus walks through the front gate, pushing Damian in the pushchair, I watch them go up the street before closing the door. Now for a nice cup of tea and a few chocolate digestive biscuits while I chat with Crystal, that's if she hasn't done one of her maniac vanishing acts.

Walking past, I notice she's sitting on the sofa, staring into space. I can sense thoughts stirring in her mind, but not in a bad way. Leaving her for a brief moment, I head into the kitchen and switch the kettle on to boil. I gert a cup and a small plate from the cupboard, then open the biscuit tin to see the delicious chocolate digestives staring back at me. Laughing to myself, I pick a couple out and place them on the plate before fetching the milk from the fridge.

The kettle clicks as it finishes boiling. I pour the hot water into my cup and add some milk, then return the kettle to its stand and place the milk back in the fridge. With everything sorted, I head off to the living room to chat with Crystal.

"Are you alright, Crystal? When I passed by on my way to the kitchen, I noticed you looked deep in thought."

"Oh yeah, I'm doing alright thanks Julia. Just thinking about tonight. It's getting closer, and we are going to kick that dark spirit back to where it came from!!"

"Good, glad you're ok. We shall indeed."

"Shall I meet you at the zoo tonight Julia, or travel in the car with you?"

Growing Up With Secrets

"It's up to you Crystal. Depends if you're going to do anything beforehand."

"Not currently. I'll come with you in the car tonight, then we can get this situation resolved once and for all."

"We sure can. It won't know what hit it once it enters the binding circle later."

"I'll do my vanishing technique like we planned."

"Indeed, that's a key part of our plan. If you do it in bursts while running, it should confuse the spirit."

"Don't worry. I'll do exactly that."

After finishing our conversation, I decide to turn on the TV while waiting for the boys to return from the park. We'll be going out for a lovely lunch at the local café just down the street.

Something catches our attention as we see a few crows flying past. A moment later, two of them land on the window ledge, and suddenly, an eerie wave of negative energy fills the room. I get up and move towards the window to shoo them away. When, out of nowhere, the dark spirit appears.

It startles us both, and I jump back in shock as it comes straight through the window into the living room.

"THIS IS YOUR FINAL WARNING. DO NOT ATTEMPT TO INTERFERE WITH MY PLANS, YOU WEAK AND FEEBLE HUMANS!!"

Before I have the chance to say anything, the dark spirit vanishes along with the crows, as if nothing had happened. Oh my goodness, that was terrifying.

Crystal and I sit there, a little shaken by what just occurred. Could this possibly be linked to the premonition I had? Has the spirit somehow realised we're coming to stop it?

It takes a few moments for us to calm down. The whole encounter was so unexpected, but looking over at Crystal, I can see the shift in her energy. She's fired up and ready for battle.

"Aghhh! How dare it scare us like that! It had better watch out. We're coming to defeat it! That dark spirit doesn't know who it's dealing with!!"

"Crystal, calm down. I understand how you feel, and we will seal it away tonight, once and for all. But we must not be reckless."

"Sorry about that Julia, I just got so annoyed after what happened!"

"It's alright, don't worry. We have a solid plan to help us succeed."

"WOOOOHOOOO!"

Growing Up With Secrets

"Go get some rest for now Crystal. I'll give you a call when it's time to leave later."

"I will do Julia. See you in a bit."

Here we go again, she vanishes just a second before I get the chance to say anything to her.

Although, if magical powers were real, I could disappear and reappear in different places with just a thought. How amazing that would be! Life would be delightfully easier without the worry of driving. Of course, if that ever happened, I'd have to keep it secret, no one could know.

That's just a fantasy, though and wishful thinking. I laugh to myself.

The boys shouldn't be long now, just another half hour to go. I'll keep busy pottering around the house for a bit, then we can all head out to the café for some well deserved lunch.

I don't realise how quickly half an hour has passed. Mind you, they always say time flies when you're busy.

I then hear the front door open as the boys arrive back home from the park. Sounds like they had a great time. I'll give them about twenty minutes before we head out to the café, when Marcus wants to go.

Daniel Cory & Charleine Shepherd

"Heymum, what fun we had over at the park! Are you ready to go for lunch at the café?"

"Hiii son. I was going to give you both twenty minutes to have a break before we head out again. Do you want to go now?"

"Let's head out Mum. I'm getting a little hungry."

"Ohhh son, thought I'd let you know the dark spirit paid me and Crystal a visit when we were sitting in the living room."

"Are you both alright?"

"Yes, we're ok son. It just warned us again not to interfere, which spooked us. Afterwards, when it was gone, Crystal had a strange burst of energy!"

"Oh right… why was that?"

"She said we will defeat it. I did explain that we have to remain vigilant. I have to admire her determination most of all."

"I certainly agree with you there mum. Let's make a move and get some lunch."

Getting up out of the armchair, I walk out of the living room to get my jacket and bag. I notice the boys are already standing there, waiting to go out. Flipping heck.

Just as Marcus opens the front door, taking Damian out in his pushchair and down the pathway, I follow behind them, closing and

Growing Up With Secrets

locking up the front door before heading down the path to the front of our drive, where the boys are waiting for me.

We head up the street while the weather seems quite nice withythe sun shining, a light breeze in the air. I take a quick glance at the fields, thinking, *Wow, what a lovely view*, as I spot some of the animals belonging to the local farm.

Reaching the end of our street, the café comes into view on the other side of the road. At the crossing, I push the button and wait for the lights to change to green. I can feel my hunger growing, my stomach starts rumbling.

Luckily, the next moment, the green man appears, signalling for us to cross the main road. Once we reach the other side, we walk slightly to the left, arriving at the café. I'm still wondering what I'm going to have, though I'm sure Marcus has already made up his mind. When it comes to food, there's not much fuss with him. He's like a walking eating machine when he has an appetite!

Opening the door to the café, we walk in and just before we take a seat. I bring over a highchair and place it at the end of the table while Marcus unclips the straps, picks Damian up, and settles him into the highchair.

As I take my seat, I grab both an adult's and a child's menu. All of a sudden, I fancy a jacket potato with some salad on the side and a cold glass of Diet Coke.

Looking over the children's menu, I decide to order Damian some fish fingers, chips, and beans with a Ribena juice carton.

A waiter comes over to take our order.

"Hello, what would you like to order?"

"Hi, please can I order the fish fingers, chips, and beans for my grandson, and a jacket potato with cheese and beans with salad for myself? Son, what are you ordering? Let the lady know when you're ready."

"Will do mum, I've just made up my mind. Please could I order the cheese quarter-pounder meal?"

"Of course. Would you like any drinks?"

"Yes please. Could we have a Diet Coke, a Ribena juice carton, and a Pepsi? That's all we'd like to order for now, thank you."

"No problem at all. I'll bring your drinks over in just a moment."

The waitress walks away towards the kitchen, handing our order through the window hatch so the chef can start preparing our food. She then heads over to the drinks section, taking two clean glasses off the

Growing Up With Secrets

shelf. She picks up a can of Diet Coke, a can of Pepsi, and a Ribena carton from the fridge, then makes her way back to us.

"Here are your drinks. Your food should be ready shortly. If there's anything else you need, please feel free to ask."

"Thank you so much."

"You're very welcome."

Crystal appears next to Marcus out of the blue of nowhere again. *Here we go again*, I think. *Here she is, the Swift Vanisher has arrived.* I have a quick two second chuckle to myself.

She hasn't really said anything, just started entertaining Damian bless her heart. I can see how happy he gets, filled with so much excitement. Marcus sits quietly, reading through the newspaper while we wait for the food to arrive. At the same time, I wonder if the waitress or anyone else here notices Damian giggling at nothing. It might make them think, *What's going on?* Ha ha.

I notice that the cuddly toy is in the pushchair, so I get it out and place it beside Damian in the highchair, giving him something to play with if he wants to. I glance over at Marcus, who has a small smirk on his face. He can hear spirits now, which I really think is amazing. Wait until he starts to see them, that will be a completely different experience. It takes time to understand the different spirits that come through.

Situations I've been involved in while dealing with spirits have varied, especially when I think about the time mother and Crystal were chased by that man in the old house we pass by on our street. Not that any of us take the slightest bit of notice of it anymore.

I look over and see the waitress heading this way with our food. The smell is amazing. I can't wait to eat now because it's making me feel even hungrier. Ha ha.

"Here are your burger meal, jacket potato, and child's meal."

"Thank you so much."

"Is there anything else I can get for you?"

"No, thank you. Everything you've done for us has been great so far."

"You're all very welcome."

The waitress walks away, heading back over to the main counter to serve another customer who looks ready to pay.

Just then, I see Crystal vanish again, even though the boys are busy eating their lunch. Time for me to start eating mine too.

Growing Up With Secrets

We have all finished eating our lunch, thinking that was really delicious, but filling too. I had thought about ordering a small dessert for each of us, perhaps some ice cream, but letting our food go down first is most important while we finish off our drinks. I'll ask Marcus what he thinks, whether we should get one each or just head back home after paying for lunch.

"Son, do you fancy a dessert, or should we head off home after paying?"

"To be fair mum, I'm full after eating that amazing burger meal. We could head home for sure after. Lunch is on me today, I'll pay."

"Aww, that's sweet of you to pay. Are you sure? I can put some money towards it."

"No, it's okay mum. This one's on me!"

"Thank you so much son."

"You are very welcome mum. I'll go pay, then we can head home."

Marcus gets up from the table and walks over to the main counter, where the waitress is standing behind the till, so he can pay for lunch. I get up quickly to put on my coat while Damian finishes the last of his Ribena. I can see he's enjoying it, but a moment later, I hear the familiar sound of an empty carton as he picks up his cuddly tiger toy. I put on his jacket, then lift him from the highchair and place him back

Daniel Cory & Charleine Shepherd

into the pushchair, securing the straps just as Marcus returns from the counter and picks up his jacket from the back of the chair.

We head out of the café, walking back to the crossing. I press the button while we wait for the crossing light to turn green so we can safely cross the main road. After about two minutes, the signal changes from red to green, and we hear the familiar beeping noise, signalling that it's safe to cross.

As we walk across the main road, I suddenly notice a strange spirit walking down the street, seemingly oblivious to everyone around him. Looks like he's from the early 1800s, although the energy I sense from him strongly suggests the year 1869, especially judging by his clothing. The next moment, he vanishes without a trace. *He must have been searching for someone for a very long time...* I get a strong sense of distress and heartbreak, like he's searching for a long lost love.

To be honest, this does tend to happen with many earthbound spirits who get stuck in a replay loop, not realising they've died until a gifted person like myself helps them find peace by crossing over to the light. This isn't always an easy task for some spirits I've encountered, having been rather difficult to move on.

I decide not to mention anything to Marcus about seeing this spirit wandering down the street. For now, he can't see spirits, he can only hear them.

Growing Up With Secrets

Looking down at Damian, I see he's already fast asleep in the pushchair as we near home. That's fine, my little man can have a short nap. Once we get back indoors, I'll lay him on the sofa with a blanket over him.

As we walk down our street, passing the old creepy house, Marcus and I both hear screaming and banging coming from inside. We glance at each other, thinking, *What on earth is going on in there?*

I look towards the house and see Crystal peering through the upstairs window, shouting for me. Then, two windows over, I spot the male spirit running quickly towards where she is.

"JULIAAA, HELP ME QUICK!!!"

"Mum, what on earth is going on? That was Crystal calling for you, she sounded distressed."

"I know son. Goodness knows what she's got herself into now. You take Damian home, I need to deal with this."

"Ok, be careful. We'll see you at home."

Heading through the gate, I run towards the back entrance, the same way I first gained access to the property when completing that spirit rescue with mother and Crystal. I dread to think what the silly girl has got herself into this time. *What on earth is she doing back here?* That's one of the biggest mysteries right now.

Daniel Cory & Charleine Shepherd

Entering through the back door, I see her running through one doorway into a room, followed closely by the male spirit. She reappears in the hallway, then dashes up the stairs again. The spirit doesn't sound too happy as I hear him shout:

"WHERE ARE YOU, GIRL? I WILL FIND YOU!!"

The next moment, I see him storm out of the room Crystal ran into. I stand there silently watching him before he vanishes upstairs. Quickly, I hurry after them both.

Reaching the top, I see Crystal being chased around the place, reappearing and deliberately provoking the male spirit.

"Wooohoooo, over this way spooky chops! Catch me if you can!"

Seriously? Sometimes I question what goes through her mind. Knowing this woman, she's dragging me into another mad dilemma.

Just then, something else catches my attention, a child spirit hiding around the corner, peeking out at the commotion. The moment she spots me looking at her, she vanishes. I quickly run in that direction while Crystal keeps the male spirit occupied. At least now I have a clearer idea of what's been happening.

Walking down the corridor, I see the girl peeking through a partly closed door at the end. As I approach, she moves further into the room. She seems scared but perhaps I can find out what's been going on. The

Growing Up With Secrets

last time I did the spirit rescue, she wasn't here. My feeling is she was hiding somewhere in the house, too afraid to come out for help.

Slowly, I open the door and see the little girl cowering in the corner, looking terrified.

"Hello lovely. You have nothing to worry about. My name is Julia, I've come to help."

"What do you want from me? How can you see me?"

"Don't be afraid sweetie. I have a special gift that allows me to see people who have died."

"I'm scared of the man that was chasing that lady."

"Don't worry. The lady is a good friend of mine. We are going to help you into the light."

"What is the light?"

"It's a special place where you will see your family and be safe from any danger. Come sit with me, and we can talk about what's holding you back. Or, if you prefer, you can touch my hand to show me."

"Ok. I trust you Julia. My name is Kathy Barrow."

Kathy places her hand on my arm, triggering a past vision by allowing me to see what happened the day she died, the reason she remains earthbound.

I find myself standing in the hallway of the house. Everything looks normal at first, but then my attention is drawn towards the kitchen. The light is on. A man and woman are talking, unaware that Kathy is sitting on the stairs listening. They are discussing how to explain to her that she was adopted at birth. I see the distress on her face as she overhears their conversation and she suddenly runs upstairs.

The vision shifts to the early hours of the night. The house is quiet. The family is sleeping soundly in their beds. Then, a strong smell of gas fills my senses. I realise this was the cause of their deaths.

Coming out of the vision, I now understand how Kathy died. But the identity of the male spirit looming around the house remains a mystery, one we'll have to solve another time. Right now, my priority is to help Kathy find peace and cross over. Crystal continues her cat-and-mouse game with the male spirit.

"Oh, come on, you can do better, grapple puss! What's wrong? Can't catch me? Isn't that such a shame!"

She's really giving him a run for his money, but no other spirit could do what she does.

I turn my attention back to Kathy.

Growing Up With Secrets

"Hey lovely. Thank you for showing me what happened the night you passed away. I understand this was very sudden. You must have been scared, looking back at yourself lying in bed in a forever sleep."

"Yes… It was very scary. I didn't understand what happened."

"I know sweetheart. But all you need to do now is think positive thoughts about your family. Close your eyes and listen to my voice."

"Okay… Here we go."

"Think of love. Think of your family, standing there, welcoming you back with smiles on their faces."

"I feel so relaxed… I can picture them in my mind."

"That's really good my lovely. Now, open your eyes."

"Oh wow… What is that light over there? I can see my family waving at me, calling me through!"

"It's time for you to cross over now. You're ready."

"Thank you for your help. Bye Julia."

"You're welcome lovely. Take care."

Watching Kathy walk towards the window, she turns, giving me a smile before crossing over into the light, finding peace with her family.

Now to get back to Crystal, as the commotion is still going on out there. I've never known anything to go on this long before. I run out to see her giving this male spirit a major run around, where she has learned some strange technique to mirror herself into different areas at once. As he runs one way, he realises some are decoys.

Quickly, I run past and down the stairs, calling to her saying, "Crystal quick, let's get out of here! He can't follow beyond the walls of this house."

As soon as I reach the bottom of the stairs, I run through to get out the back door. Holding it open, expecting her to follow me out, the woman appears behind me, making me jump.

"Heyyyy Julia! Well, that was so much fun."

"Barjeeze woman! What are you trying to do? Give me a flipping heart attack?!"

"Sorry about that, didn't mean to startle you. Did you manage to find that little girl spirit?"

"Yeah, I've crossed her over into the light. Well done for distracting that male spirit, although he isn't happy. But never mind, here he comes!"

"I'LL GET YOU BOTH FOR THIS, MARK MY WORDS! HOW DARE YOU COME INTO MY DOMAIN LIKE THAT? WE HAD AN AGREEMENT!" the male spirit shouts.

"Shut up Grizzly," says Crystal.

Growing Up With Secrets

"Crystal stop! Just because he's stuck in there, don't taunt him anymore. Not sure who you are, but yes, we did have an agreement. However, there was a scared little girl who needed help to cross over! Bye for now. Come on Crystal, let's go."

"Julia, what about old Grizzly Chops?"

"Leave him. We've finished what needed to be done. I have to get back home to see the boys, plus don't forget we have the dark spirit to contend with tonight."

"Yes, of course! We need to be ready for that big lump of darkness!"

"Lump of darkness?! Are you mad woman? You're giving everything a nickname! We have to be serious about tonight to get rid of this dark spirit."

"We will get rid of the dark spirit tonight. I'll use the new mirror technique to duplicate myself."

"Can't wait to get mother and Katie safe and that thing sealed away. Anyway, we're almost back at the house now, then we can go in to see the boys."

Approaching the house, I think to myself, *that was an unexpected situation to be dragged into out of nowhere.* At least the main thing is, I got Kathy crossed into the light so she can be at peace with her family.

Daniel Cory & Charleine Shepherd

Arriving back at the house, I walk up the driveway to open the front door. Crystal is already in the hallway as I walk in thinking, *this woman takes the mick, showing off just because she's a spirit, able to go from one place to another in a flash.*

Taking off my jacket, I place it back in the cupboard. After doing that, I walk into the living room to see Damian fast asleep in Marcus's arms while he watches the TV. He then looks over at me.

"Hey mum. Did everything go alright at the abandoned house where Crystal shouted out for you?"

"Hello son. Yes, it's all sorted. Turned out it was a little girl who was earthbound, wasone I must have missed the first time I went there to complete the spirit rescue."

"So pleased you managed to get the little girl crossed over into the light. You have always been amazing at how you deal with these different situations. Are you and Crystal going to deal with that dark spirit situation tonight?"

"Yes, we are indeed. Once it's sealed away, we won't have any issues, after we can get nan and Katie back safely. I'm going to sit and rest for a few hours before we have to go."

"That's a great idea mum. You need to be well rested and ready for tonight!"

Growing Up With Secrets

"Do you want to wake Damian up at 14:00? It just helps keep his sleep routine at night. I'm going to head upstairs for a couple of hours for a short rest."

"Ok mum. I'll wake the little man up at about 13:45. Have a good rest."

"Thanks son. See you both shortly."

CHAPTER 15

The alarm clock starts beeping as I turn over, looking at the time its 17:30 pm. I reach over and turn it off, stretching before getting myself up and making my way into the bathroom to freshen up.

Turning on the tap, I splash some water on my face, then dry it, feeling a bit more rejuvenated energy-wise. Time to head back downstairs to see how the boys are getting on and have a quick cup of coffee. While I'm at it, I think about how it will soon be time for me and the swift vanisher to go back to the zoo this evening to battle with the dark spirit at long last and seal the thing away. I know everything is prepped and ready to go.

Walking into the kitchen, I call out to Marcus.

"Son, would you like a coffee or tea while I'm in the kitchen?"

"Yes please mum. I'll have a cup of coffee. Could you bring a small beaker of warm milk in for Damian, please?"

"No worries son. Give me ten minutes, I'll make our coffees and do a beaker for little man."

"Thanks mum. Just shout if you need any help."

"Will do son."

I press the button on the kettle to boil while getting two cups and a beaker from the cupboard, placing a teaspoon of coffee in each. I

Growing Up With Secrets

head to the fridge, take out the bottle of milk, and return to the counter to pour some into Damian's beaker, quickly placing it in the microwave for about a minute to warm up. I put the milk back in the fridge, and just as I do, the kettle clicks. Pouring the hot water into both cups, I give them a stir. The microwave beeps, so I take the beaker out, checking to make sure it's not too hot, it turns out perfectly fine.

Picking up both cups while holding the beaker, I head back into the living room. I hand Marcus his cup of coffee before kneeling down to give Damian his beaker of milk. He's playing with his toys just as I come back in.

Sitting down in the armchair, I take a sip of my coffee, feeling ready for tonight's banishing at the zoo. I'll give Doug a call on his office number to let him know when I'm leaving home. Thinking over the plans, I'm 100% sure this will not fail, especially since I have complete confidence in my spiritual sealing knowledge. I spent years studying through various books loaned from the library at the time.

Placing my cup down on the coffee table, I lift my bag, checking all the equipment and written plans for tonight to ensure nothing is missing. I know what my memory is like at the best of times. Thankfully, everything is here. I place the bag back on the floor.

I notice Crystal appearing on the sofa next to Marcus, not saying anything, just smiling as she watches Damian. He looks up at her,

Daniel Cory & Charleine Shepherd

showing his tiger toy, and in the next moment, Marcus looks over at me to ask something.

"Mum, did you want anything to eat before you head out shortly to the zoo?"

"I wouldn't mind a sandwich please, if you don't mind making it."

"Yeah of course not mum. I can make Damian a small bowl of Heinz spaghetti bolognese before taking him up for a bath and then bed."

"Thanks son. Could you do me a ham salad sandwich, please?"

"Sure thing mum, no problem. When I give you a shout that it's ready, can you bring Damian to the kitchen too please?"

"Will do son."

Marcus heads into the kitchen to make our food. I then pick up little man off the floor after he reaches out to me, saying, "Nan, nan." Bless his heart, he's really sweet. He's going to grow up to be an amazing young man. I'll be here to help him understand how to use his gift when the time comes for him to speak with the dead.

Turning towards Crystal, I see her giving Damian some fuss and attention, it's really lovely. I quickly mention to her, "Crystal, are you all ready for tonight? Feeling up to what needs to be done with the distraction technique?"

Growing Up With Secrets

"Yes for sure Julia. No problem, I'm ready."

"Brilliant news."

She carries on making funny faces and voices, making Damian giggle. Watching them both is very amusing.

"Crystal, can you watch Damian for just a moment while I put all his toys away in the toy chest? It'll save me a job later."

"Yes, of course Julia."

While I quickly tidy away the small number of toys, Marcus calls out that our food is ready on the table and asks us to come to the kitchen. Closing the lid on the toy chest, I then pick up little man from the sofa, signalling for Crystal to follow us.

As I leave the living room, I glance back for a brief second, only to realise she's already vanished. *She'll be back shortly*, I think to myself.

***

After we finish eating, Marcus takes Damian upstairs to give him a bath before bedtime. I give my little man a quick kiss on the cheek before continuing to tidy up. I need to get ready to head out to the zoo with Crystal, but first, I'll give Doug a quick call to let him know we're on our way.

"Crystal, are you ready to go?"

"Heyy, Julia, I'm ready."

"Super. Let me give Doug a call, then we'll make a move."

Picking up the house phone, I dial Doug's direct office number at the zoo.

Ring ring Ring ring

"Hello, Doug speaking."

"Hi Doug, it's Julia Jones. Just giving you a call to say I'm leaving my house now and will be at the zoo in 30 minutes."

"Thanks for letting me know Julia. Looking forward to seeing you shortly. Take care."

"See you soon, Doug. Bye for now."

I call upstairs to Marcus.

"Son, I'm leaving to go to the zoo for this clearing."

"Ok, see you later. Take care and be careful mum."

"We will. See you soon. Bye son."

Opening the front door, I step outside and close it behind me. Looking ahead, I see Crystal already waiting in the car. Flipping heck she moves fast! She's been getting into her show off moods a lot lately.

I quickly walk down the driveway, unlock the car, and get in. Starting the engine, we pull away and make our way to the zoo. We sit quietly, listening to music, which helps distract my mind from the

Growing Up With Secrets

small doubts creeping in about sealing this dark spirit away tonight. Deep down, I know it'll be done.

Time passes quickly, and I soon spot a sign for the zoo as we approach the junction leading to the car park. I switch on the indicator, pulling onto the slip road. The car park is completely empty as I drive up to the main entrance. Parking outside, I put on the handbrake, turn off the engine, and step out of the car while Crystal simply passes straight through the car door. That ability would definitely make things easier.

Here we go.

Walking up to the main entrance, I press the buzzer, which connects to Doug's office and the main reception building. While we wait for him to open the door, Crystal turns to me.

"Julia would you be ok if I go ahead to scope the area? I'll keep my eyes open and make sure to hide if the dark spirit appears."

"Yes of course. Just be careful and meet me in the room near the lions' enclosure in 15 minutes."

"Ok, I'll meet you there and report back on what I see."

With that, Crystal vanishes, heading off to check the zoo grounds and track the dark spirit's movements.

A moment later, Doug opens the door.

Daniel Cory & Charleine Shepherd

"Hello Julia. Nice to see you. Please, come through."

"Hi Doug. Thank you. If it's ok, I'd like to head straight to the lions' enclosure storage cupboard to get started."

"Of course, please do. You know where my office is, just pop in after you're finished."

"Thanks Doug. See you later."

I head towards the lions' enclosure to set up the sealing circle to trap the dark spirit. Crystal should be on her way there now with an update on its whereabouts.

As I walk past the dolphin show centre, I suddenly spot the dark spirit near the zoo café. It's in human form, moving through the wall into another building. My heart pounds. I need to get to the storage room quickly, set things up, and let Crystal know I've seen it lurking.

Round the corner, I see the door in sight, and Crystal standing outside waiting for me.

"Juliaaa, what's wrong?"

"I just saw the dark spirit walking by. It didn't see me."

"Ok, as long as you're alright."

"Yes I'm fine. Let's get inside so I can draw the sealing circle."

Growing Up With Secrets

Opening the storage room door, we both step inside, closing it behind us. I place my bag on the floor, reach inside, and pull out a stick of white chalk. Kneeling down, I begin drawing the sealing circle.

I carefully place six white candles around the circle, evenly spaced. Striking a match, I light each one before reciting the barrier incantation. A pure white energy begins forming the circle, this will prevent the dark spirit from escaping once it enters.

"Crystal, are you ready to lure the dark spirit this way?"

"LET'S DO THIS! WOOO!!!"

"Calm down woman! Jeez, overexcited much? When you run back this way towards the door, just keep going straight through. The dark spirit will follow and step directly into the circle, getting caught. It won't affect you."

"I'll watch from afar to make sure you're ok. Let's go get this done!"

Crystal vanishes like the wind, heading straight to where the dark spirit was last lurking near the café. Knowing her, this is going to turn into one massive circus ground when she starts taunting it.

I walk over to stand behind another enclosure, keeping an eye out for when things kick off. A few moments later, a massive roar echoes through the zoo. Suddenly, I see Crystal sprinting across the grounds, the dark spirit now in its beast form chasing after her. Seconds later, she reappears on the other side, shouting, "Yooohoo, dampen chops! Over this way!"

As it starts moving towards her, she vanishes again, only to reappear in a different spot. I feel a wave of anxiety as the dark spirit locks eyes on her once more.

The next moment, she uses her spirit mirror duplication technique, making it look as though she's everywhere at once. Her duplicates scatter in all directions, frustrating the dark spirit as it roars in confusion. The illusion lasts only a few seconds before she reappears near the storage room, shouting, "Wooohooooo! You lovely lump of darkness, this way come get me!"

The creature looks utterly vicious, its red eyes glowing with fury. It lets out a thunderous roar before bellowing, "I'LL HAVE YOUR SOUL FOR THIS! YOU'RE GOING TO BE MINE, GIRL! AGHHHH!!!"

It charges straight for her, oblivious to the trap lying ahead. As it speeds past me, Crystal sprints through the storage room door, with the dark spirit following her. The moment it crosses the threshold, the seal barrier is triggered. A bright light flares up from beneath the door, confirming the trap has sprung.

Crystal suddenly appears next to me, grinning.

Growing Up With Secrets

"The lovely dark lump is caught in the barrier, just like you planned. And now it's screaming to be let out! Hahaha!"

"Well done Crystal! That was brilliant work. We caught the dark spirit. Let's go seal this thing away for good!"

"Wooo! Let's go, sealing time!"

Together, we walk back to the storage room. As I open the door, we see the dark spirit thrashing against the barrier wall, its massive form seething with rage. It's desperately trying to break free, but the seal is already draining its negative energy. I smirk, knowing it's futile.

I reach into my bag and pull out the sealing incantation scroll. Once activated, it will summon light chains to encase the dark spirit, dragging it back to the demon realm, never to return.

"SILLY HUMAN! YOU CAN'T SEAL ME AWAY! WHEN I GET FREE, I'LL TAKE ALL YOUR SOULS!!!"

"Ohhh, shut up. You're not taking anything. FYI, you'll be sealed within the next five minutes!"

The dark spirit continues its futile attempts to break through the barrier, but it's impenetrable.

I begin chanting the sealing incantation. White light erupts from the circle as luminous chains shoot out, wrapping around the beast. It thrashes violently, roaring in agony as its power is drained. I keep chanting, watching as the final part of the spell takes effect. The creature is dragged downward, sucked into the glowing seal, back to where it belongs in the demon realm.

Within a minute, it's gone.

The moment the seal closes, all the candles blow out simultaneously. It's done.

I take a damp cloth and wipe away the chalk markings. That's one part finished. Now, we need to find mother and Crystal, who were trapped in that energy cage. Thankfully, breaking it should be much easier.

A faint voice calls out from a larger room at the back of the complex.

"Julia, is that you darling?"

"Yes mum, it's me! Hold on, we're coming to set you both free."

"It's so good to see you again. It feels like we've been here forever! Poor Katie hasn't been herself since, she's just sitting in the corner."

"Don't worry mum. It's the energy cage affecting her. It's suppressing the light energy around you both. But don't worry, we'll get you out now."

I take out two obsidian crystals and place them on either side of the energy cage. Channelling my energy into them disrupts the cage's

Growing Up With Secrets

structure, causing it to dissolve and absorb the negative energy. Within seconds, the barrier disappears, and both mother and Katie are free.

I immediately go to Katie and place my hands on her, sending healing energy into her body. A warm glow surrounds her, and after a few moments, she looks up at me, smiling. She's already starting to brighten up, looking more like her usual self.

She's safe now.

Now, the last thing I need to do is help Katie find peace and cross into the light. But first, she needs to speak with her mum so they can both find closure.

I watch as mother, Crystal, and Katie vanish together. Relief comes over me, knowing they're safe. I'll speak with them later. For now, I need to see Doug and let him know that everything has been completed with the problem is now finished.

I leave the storage room, closing the door behind me, and make my way back towards the main office building opposite the reception. It's only a short walk, and I can already see the building ahead.

Reaching the door, I open it and step inside. Walking down the corridor, I stop in front of Doug's office and knock.

"Come on in Julia."

I enter and give him a reassuring nod.

"Hello Doug. Just wanted to let you know everything's been sorted. The zoo staff will be able to work in peace now. Oh I almost forgot the archive files are still at home. Are you in any rush for me to return them?"

"No major hurry Julia. Bring them back whenever you're next passing by."

"Super. I'll drop them off at reception tomorrow on my way through."

"That's great. And thank you for everything you've done."

"You're very welcome Doug. I'd best get home now and get some rest. It's been a tough evening."

"No problem. Allow me to see you out."

"Thank you."

Doug gets up from his desk, where I notice piles of paperwork, likely for upcoming events and signing off invoices for stock arriving at the zoo. They need to feed the animals, after all. We head through the door, walking down the corridor and back out into the main complex. He leads me towards the back door, the same one he let me in through earlier this evening.

Opening the door that leads to the car park, he steps aside for me to exit. We shake hands before parting ways. When I reach my car, I

Growing Up With Secrets

unlock it, open the door, and get in. Starting the engine, I pull out of the car park and back onto the main dual carriageway, reflecting on what a crazy evening it has been. At least it's all finished now. The exhaustion is catching up with me, and I know I'll be going straight to bed when I get home.

After what feels like a long drive, I finally reach home. Pulling up outside the house, I turn off the engine, get out, and lock the car. As I walk down the driveway past Marcus's car, I reach the front door, place the key in the lock, and step inside.

"Hi son, I'm back. Are you alright?"

"Hey mum. All good. Damian's already in bed, I put him down not long after you left. How did it all go?"

"It was very tiring, but we sealed it away for good. I'm going to head to bed, son."

"No problem mum. See you in the morning."

"Goodnight son."

Walking out of the living room, I head upstairs. Before going to bed, I decide to check in on the little man to make sure he's ok. Reaching the top of the stairs, I step into Damian's room and notice the night light glowing softly, giving the space a warm and safe feel.

Daniel Cory & Charleine Shepherd

Peering into the cot, I see him sleeping soundly, his toy tiger tucked under the duvet.

Satisfied that he's fine, I quietly leave the room, leaving the door slightly ajar. Entering my own room, I change into my pyjamas, pull back the duvet, and climb into bed. With a tired sigh, I switch off the bedside lamp, finally ready for some well deserved rest.

Marcus wakes me early at 7:00 am, letting me know he's heading off to work after his short break. Even though I'm still half asleep, I hear his voice clearly.

"Mum wake up. I'm heading off to work now. See you later."

"Mmm... No problem son. See you later. Have a good day."

Briefly opening my eyes, I watch him walk out of my room, heading downstairs and out the front door. I hear it click shut behind him.

I decide I might as well get up. Heading to the bathroom, I get washed and dressed before checking on Damian. I can already hear him giggling, which is unusual for this early in the morning. I suspect Marcus must have checked on him before leaving.

Just as I open the bathroom door, I hear Crystal's voice coming from Damian's bedroom. Curious, I quickly peek around the door and see her performing her vanishing and reappearing tricks to entertain him. Shaking my head with a small smile, I continue getting ready.

Growing Up With Secrets

Once dressed, I step into Damian's room.

"Good morning little man, and good morning Crystal. Looks like you're both having loads of fun! Let's get you ready for your first day at nursery."

"Morninngggg Julia!" Crystal replies cheerfully.

I dress Damian in fresh clothes, placing his pyjamas neatly on the edge of his cot. Then we all head downstairs, though as expected, Crystal vanishes in an instant, likely appearing straight in the kitchen to show off. I chuckle to myself as I follow behind with Damian in my arms.

As I reach the bottom of the stairs, I hear her calling for me from the kitchen.

"Juliaaaaaa, where are youuuu?"

I roll my eyes and shout back, "Shut it woman! I'm coming, hold your horses will ya? Jeez!"

Damian giggles at our exchange, his laughter brightening the morning. Entering the kitchen, I place him in his high chair before heading to the cupboard to get out the Weetabix, coffee, a bowl, and a cup.

247

Daniel Cory & Charleine Shepherd

Noticing the kettle has just finished boiling, I realise Crystal must have clicked the button. Well, that saves me a job, I think as I scoop a teaspoon of coffee into my mug.

I prepare Damian's breakfast and place it in front of him, watching as he eagerly starts eating. Thankfully, he loves Weetabix. I take a seat, sipping my coffee, mentally preparing for the last task of the day that involves speaking with Katie's mum. She needs to know her daughter is still here in spirit, and I need to give her closure before helping Katie move into the light.

It's early, but I remind myself that Damian needs to be at nursery by 8:45 am for early drop off. He'll meet his new teacher and classmates today. Checking the time, I see it's only 7:55 am—plenty of time.

After breakfast, I place the washing up in the sink to soak, then dry my hands before picking Damian up from his high chair. Carrying him into the living room, I let him play with his toys while I settle down with the newspaper, taking a few quiet moments before we head out for the day.

Looking over at the clock sitting on the mantelpiece, I see it's already 8:20 am. Right, best to get ready to go, I think to myself. I get mine and Damian's shoes along with our coats, putting them on us both before clearing away his toys into the box. Picking up his small

Growing Up With Secrets

lunchbox and the car keys, I lift Damian into my arms and walk out into the hallway, opening the front door.

As we step outside, I close the door behind us, locking it. Just then, I realise my car is in the driveway. Marcus must have moved them around before he left for work. That makes things a little easier, I think as I walk up to the passenger side. Unlocking and opening the car door, I place Damian into his car seat, only to notice Crystal already sitting next to him in the back. Wowww.

Once Damian is securely strapped in, I close the door and walk around to the driver's side, getting into the car and starting the engine. Ready to pull off the driveway, I head down the road towards *Star & Moon Nursery*. Thankfully, it's only a five-minute drive. As we go, I hear Crystal and Damian giggling away in the back.

Reaching the nursery, I enter the car park and pull into one of the free bays. I see a few other parents dropping off their children early, likely on their way to work. Turning off the engine, I pick up Damian's lunchbox and open my door to get out. Walking around to the back, I unstrap Damian, lift him out of his car seat, and close the door behind us.

Making our way to the reception entrance, we are warmly greeted by one of the nursery staff.

"Good morning, welcome to the *Star & Moon Nursery*. My name is Serena, I'm one of the teaching assistants. And who is this?"

"Hello Serena, lovely to meet you. My name is Julia, and this is my grandson Damian. It's his first day today."

"Oh wonderful! I can see he's really excited to be here. Would you like me to take him through for you?"

"That's so kind of you. Yes please. This is Damian's lunchbox for later. Right, little man be good, and nanny will see you this afternoon."

"We'll see you later, Julia."

"Thank you! Bye for now."

Walking back out into the car park, I notice Crystal already sitting in the front seat of the car, throwing strange looks in the direction of Serena. As I approach the car, I open the door, get in, and start the engine before turning to Crystal.

"What on earth were you giving Serena funny looks for? She can't even see you!"

"OMG, did you see the state of her? Like, what was she wearing?"

"What do you mean, *look at the state of her*?"

"She dresses like my nan used to when she was alive!"

"You're so rudeee. Pack it up!"

Growing Up With Secrets

Crystal just sits there now, staring out the window with a grin on her face as if nothing was said. Well, time to make a move, I think to myself. Next stop is Katie's mum's house, where I can explain the whole situation and pass on any messages Katie has for her before we send her peacefully into the light.

Pulling out of the parking bay, I drive out of the car park, turning left onto the main road, making my way towards Katie's mum's house.

***

We arrive outside Katie's mum's house, but neither Crystal nor I can sense any energy of Katie's presence. Did she go with my mother after we rescued them both? That's my first thought, but I'm not sure where they went, as Crystal hasn't said anything to me yet.

Getting out of the car, I head towards the front gate, opening it and walking up the pathway to ring the doorbell. I hear someone approaching, and a shadow moves behind the small side window to the left. A moment later, the door opens.

"Hello, may I help you?"

"Hi, my name is Julia Jones. I've come regarding your daughter, Katie."

"What about my daughter? Just so you're aware, she passed away some time ago."

Daniel Cory & Charleine Shepherd

"Would it be alright if I came inside? I need to go over a few things I've found out that might bring you some closure around her death."

"Yes, of course. Please come in Julia. My name is Sandra, let's go through to the living room and sit down. I can make us a cup of tea with some biscuits."

"Thank you Sandra. It's lovely to meet you, and that sounds great."

Walking into Sandra's house as she invites me in, I head straight to the living room, and she follows close behind. I can see the distressed look on her face. She's already bracing herself for whatever I'm about to say about her daughter. This will be a tough conversation, especially since I can see Katie due to my gift of speaking with the dead.

"Please, have a seat Julia. Let me just go make us a cup of tea. How do you like it?"

"Thank you. Please can I have it with milk and two sugars?"

"Of course, I'll be right back."

Watching Sandra head off to the kitchen to make the tea and get some biscuits, mother and Katie suddenly pop in out of nowhere, while Crystal sits next to me on the sofa. Right on time. They must have already known we were here, even after I mentioned I would speak to Katie's mum to pass on any messages.

252

Growing Up With Secrets

"Sorry honey, that we didn't tell you where we were. It didn't cross my mind. Are you both alright?"

"Yes, we're good mum. Sandra has just gone into the kitchen to make us a cup of tea. I haven't told her about my gift yet."

"Ok, no problem. You're really good at explaining your gift."

Sandra walks back in carrying a small tray with two cups and a plate of mixed biscuits. Now that Katie is here, it's time to explain my gift and hopefully bring some peace to what happened. I have a strong hunch that Sandra already knows about the incident at the zoo when the training session went terribly wrong.

"Here you go, Julia. Hope that's okay for you. Please help yourself to a biscuit. So, you had something to tell me about Katie?"

"Thank you. Yes, I do. I know this might sound strange, but I have a gift that allows me to speak with spirits. I've spoken to Katie's spirit, she has remained what I call earthbound, unable to find closure, which has stopped her from crossing into the light."

"Oh my… is she here with us now?"

"Yes, she's standing next to you. She wants to say sorry for what happened to her at the zoo during her training session with the orca whale."

"Oh my God… she really is here! Hello darling. It's not your fault what happened in your show. It was explained to me that the orca whale had some problems of its own. I love and miss you so much, things aren't the same without you here Katie."

"Don't worry, she can hear everything you're saying to her. Katie says she feels guilty because she never got to apologise after a small disagreement you both had. She stormed out of the house that day, saying, 'I'm going to work,' and it was never settled."

"I want you to understand it was never your fault, honey. Please know that I love you very much, and you're amazing. I've been thinking about you every day since the accident, and I still have that photo up on the wall of us from our day out at the beach."

I watch as Katie wipes the tears from her mum's face. Sandra closes her eyes for a moment, and I can see she feels her daughter's presence. A wave of comfort comes over her, knowing that closure is finally within reach.

"Katie says that day at the beach is something she will treasure always, and she loves you with all her heart."

Katie suddenly turns, her gaze drawn towards something beyond us.

"Julia, what is that light over there? Is that for me? I see my Grandad and Nanna waving at me, smiling."

Growing Up With Secrets

"Yes, that's for you lovely. That means you're ready."

I turn to Sandra. "Katie can see the light, she's ready to cross over."

Tears well up in Sandra's eyes. "Ohhh, my darling Katie, please always remember I love you so much. You're my wonderful daughter."

Katie leans in, giving her mum one final kiss on the cheek. Sandra instinctively places her hand over her left cheek, tears rolling down her face, but there's a smile there too. She knows her daughter is finally finding peace.

Katie reappears near the window, turning to say her final farewell.

"Julia, thank you so much for everything. Please look after my mum."

And with that, she steps into the light and vanishes.

I take a deep breath and turn to Sandra. "She's crossed over now. She wanted to say one last goodbye."

Sandra wipes her eyes. "Julia, thank you so much for everything you've done today."

"You're very welcome. Here's my number if you ever need anything, please don't hesitate to call. We'll stay in touch, and we can meet up for a regular catch up. Just know that Katie is finally at peace now."

"I'll stay in touch. Let me walk you out."

We both stand, and I give Sandra a comforting hug. These situations are always difficult for families, but at least this has bought some closure. Walking out of the living room, I step outside, waving goodbye as Sandra stands in the doorway.

Crystal and mother are already waiting by the car, both with massive grins on their faces. Oh, great… what are they plotting now?

I shake my head, knowing whatever it is will no doubt lead to more diabolical situations. Goodness help me.

Just as I reach the car, they both vanish. Sighing, I unlock the door, get inside, and start the engine. I give Sandra a final smile and wave as I pull away driving up the road.

Join Julia and the gang soon for more adventures in the next book: *Growing Up with Secrets: Part 2* **– Coming Soon!**

Printed in Great Britain
by Amazon